A Pirate's Wife

By

Lynelle Clark

1

Copyright 2012 by Lynelle Clark

A Pirate's Wife Original E-Book
Editor Mary C Findley
Cover Design by Truth Designs
E-Book ISBN 9780620527064

Self-Published: Lynelle Clark
Copyright © Lynelle Clark 2019
Editor Isak de Lange
Paperback book cover design by
Milk Tee Designs by Fionn Jameson
Paper back ISBN 978-0-620-81100-2
Print on demand.

Printing and binding by:
Groep 7 Printers and Publishers (Pty)Ltd
Pretoria, www.groep7.co.za
epos@groep7.co.za

Dedication

To all the authors who inspired me allowing me a moment of joy as I explored their Worlds of imagination. Especially Ena Murray, a well-known South African writer. Her stories were the motivation for this book.

My children; I love you guys.

To Mary C. Findley who helped with the proof reading and polishing of this, my first book. Thank you for your patience; your knowledge impacted my writing greatley. What a blessing you have become.

To Isak, thanks for your support and help with the final read of the book for printing. Your insight is much appreciated.

Contents

Title
Copyright
Dedication
Prologue
Chapter 1
Chapter 2
Chapter 3
Chapter 4
Chapter 5
Chapter 6
Chapter 7
Chapter 8
Chapter 9
Chapter 10
Chapter 11
Chapter 12
Chapter 13
Chapter 14
Chapter 15
Chapter 16
Chapter 17
Chapter 18
Chapter 19
Chapter 20
Chapter 21
Chapter 22
Authors History

Proverbs 1:1-33

The proverbs of Solomon, son of David, king of Israel: To know wisdom

and instruction, to understand words of insight, to receive instruction in wise

dealing, in righteousness, justice, and equity; to give prudence to the

simple, knowledge and discretion to the youth— Let the wise hear and

increase in learning, and the one who understands obtain guidance, ...

Prologue

It was Christmas of 1623 when six people stepped onto the dock at the harbour of Lisbon, Portugal. It was a cloudless, sunny day with a definite bite of cold in the air. People scattered around the harbour, pulling jackets tight to keep body heat in, each busy with luggage, hauling crates off various colossal wooden hull ships. Each had three masts rigged with sail and heavy tackle and supplies, ready for trade to new destinations. Sailors shouted at each other, in anger or in banter, in their usual sailors' dialect, accompanied by loud and heavy thuds as the gigantic ships were either unloaded or reloaded, depending whether they arrived or were departing on a new course.

In between the shouting of the sailors, animals bellowed, clucked or whinnied, waiting for attention. Everyone raced to finish so that they could go to the already awaiting soiled doves waving seductively to the tired but aroused sailors. Their half-clad bodies teased men hungry for female companionship after six months or more at sea.

No one gave the group of six passing by much thought, because they looked like ordinary citizens. Led by a tall blond man, the two women of the group were attracting a few lustful looks of unwanted characters. The men protected them though, guiding them through the throng to a waiting carriage ready to take them to their destination.

They had lost everything of earthly value but discovered who they were as human beings. They were survivors of the vast untamed Continent of Africa, overcoming the greatest odds against them, gaining new friends and unlikely love. The company consisted of the stout blond sailor and his old sailor friend, the Contessa who held a little girl by the hand, the sea captain, and a slave girl. Bone weary, they entered the carriage. The blond giant closed the door behind them, tapping on the roof to signal the coach driver to move.

He wrapped the frail body of the beautiful black-haired Contessa Qonchita in his steely arms. Rosa-Lee, the little girl, slept in her mother's arms. The gentle giant gazed at her with love and adoration. One thick finger caressed the soft pink cheek of the little girl he had accepted as his own. Cisco's thoughts back to where their journey had begun.

Two years ago, they had embarked on a voyage from India to Portugal, a supposedly easy and hassle-free voyage. But it had tested their endurance and their faith in the Hand of Providence and in each other.

†††

Qonchita - September 12, 1621

We have finally arrived on the ship Armando *on our long-awaited journey. Five years I stayed in this hell hole. Finally, I am leaving, a disillusioned wife and mother. Rosa-Lee is the only highlight of it all, born out of abuse, but a shining beacon in my life.*

The sea seemed to be calm enough and Captain Laurenco Breno assured us that our voyage would be without problems. That remains to be seen since the ocean could change instantly.

I didn't like the captain's beady eyes, his expression cold and stormy, with a glimmer of evil in the black depths. His lustful eyes raked over me and I felt violated by this act. I had to stop myself from shivering in front of this obnoxious man and will keep my distance the entire trip.

Rosa-Lee made a friend today. It was the first time I saw her openly speaking to an older man as she did to the giant sailor, with such familiarity. I hope we don't cause him any trouble. The look of disdain from the captain towards the blond sailor was undeniably menacing.

I never saw such a big man. His tanned, hard body stretched his white cotton shirt, his height towering over all on the boat including Faro, who is not short at all. But he was kind to Rosa-Lee, humble in his approach. Careful, maybe, with only a slight smile on the handsome face caused by her continuous chatter. There is something different in him. I find myself standing close to observe him better, something I have never done with any man, not even my own husband. Faro calls me "ice princess" and I like to I keep it that way.

I hope I can see the sailor again.

Qonchita shut the old leather-bound diary, set the pen down, and crept under the soft blankets of the bed in the cabin appointed to her and Rosa-Lee, already in a deep sleep. She brushed the dark locks of her daughter and kissed the rosy cheeks.

"I love you," she whispered to the small child, and lying back she prayed softly for a safe voyage.

†††

Cisco - September 12, 1621

New people boarded the ship today: a man and his wife and their young child. The chatter of the little girl was interesting to say the least. I never thought I would love her attention so much. What would the fellows say if they hear about this? Big Cisco Almaida falling for a little girl's kindness.

She stood next to her mother, a striking woman with dark hair coiffed perfectly. The eyes were shadowed as if to hide something deeper. She was not happy, even if she was married to the rich merchant. Faro Iago's reputation preceded him. How could she be married to that scoundrel, who was far beneath her? The man clearly did not appreciate her or his daughter.

How many times have I wished for a wife and child of my own? Like this man had. After nineteen years on this ship it was only a dream, but the little girl did something today. She touched a very deep desire for a family of my own. Maybe even a piece of land where I could retire. An impossible dream for any hardened sailor.

Can I be so bold to continue this dream?

Cisco sighed and closed his eyes. The hammock swayed with the gentle movements of the ocean. A sway he hardly noticed anymore. He touched his fingers to his forehead, then to each side of his chest, and prayed silently to the God he had learnt to trust above anything else.

✝✝✝

Trapped in a marriage arranged by her father with a cold-hearted older man, Faro Iago, Qonchita had no way to escape. The business transaction had been profitable to both parties. Faro did not care for her or for his four-year-old daughter. The fragile lady admired Cisco. Since they boarded, Faro Iago had made a beeline for the captain's cabin which housed the best of everything, including fine whiskey.

Immediately drawn to the gentle giant, the little girl, spitting image of her mother, accepted him first as a friend, and then as her new father. Daily Rosa-Lee would seek him out; with Qonchita always close by and under much scrutiny of Captain Breno.

✝✝✝

Qonchita - *September 13, 1621*

Again, we spent time with Cisco today. Rosa-Lee simply cannot leave him alone. At first, he was reluctant to encourage her, tending to his work at hand. But her constant chatter put a smile on his face and by lunch he talked to her softly. I could see his eyes were always seeking the captain.

I found Faro with some of the sailors gambling and it made me uneasy, but I kept quiet and spent my day with Rosa-Lee. To speak out of turn is unheard off.

I understand we are three hundred and forty-eight people in all, with slaves numbering two hundred. The Captain told me it was quite a large number but bragged his vessel can carry the load.

With the slaves in confinement in the hold of the ship the deck is not overcrowded but I wonder how they fair down there in this heat.

I can only hope that we will be well and that the Lord's protection will be with us daily.

†††

Cisco - September 14, 1621

The little girl's persistent chatter and continuous company gets me in trouble. The Captain warned me today for the final time. He is within his rights of course. As a sailor I know this. But how can I ignore her? She is a pleasure to have around. And her mother (he smiled thinking of the raven-head) *is gorgeous but I must keep my distance. She is married, a lady of good means. I am just a sailor. I can offer her nothing more than kindness.*

But I can dream, even if it is futile. I know it is trivial but the feelings she invokes in me make me feel worthy to love and to dream of a family of my own.

Alfonso warned me that the men are talking, that they have seen the looks we give each other. I don't want to cause her trouble. She is too much of a lady for riff-raff to speak of her in that fashion.

I will have to keep my distance and the mast would be perfect; where the little girl cannot find me. I will have to speak to Tanur tomorrow.

†††

Qonchita - *September 15, 1621*

Cisco was on the mast today. Never once did he come down to speak with Rosa-Lee. Even when she called out to him he did not look at her. I could see that it hurt her, but I had to explain to her that he must do his work. He is a sailor and cannot spend time with her. Unwilling she accepted it and played reluctantly with her doll. Her eyes fixated on the mast.

I cannot blame her; I miss his gentle ways.

Faro tried to talk to us today, but he was drunk, and Rosa-Lee feared him. He swayed on his feet, his eyes bloodshot. I heard there was trouble with the game and the Captain warned him to be careful around the sailors. Would he listen to the warnings?

I saw some of the slaves today. Met a young Indian girl. Her name is Kayla. We got to talk for a while before she had to go back into the hold. Rosa-Lee also liked her. She was very beautiful, and several sailors looked at her. I was uneasy at her common flirting with them while we talked. In the future I will be careful of her and the company she keeps.

†††

Cisco - September 16, 1621

I bumped into the lady today. It was by pure accident since I keep my distance, but when I touched her, I could not let her go. After the initial shock passed and she realized who held her she relaxed in my arms. For a few seconds I could only enjoy the lady in my arms. She fits perfectly. She is more beautiful up close. I had to struggle not to kiss her and I could see she wanted me to. That would be a mistake.

12

I know it is wrong, but I cannot help myself. The feelings I have for her are growing daily. I will have to work harder to avoid her as much as possible. A sailor and a lady are absolutely unsuited. It can never happen.

†††

Qonchita - *September 16, 1621*

I cannot believe I was in his arms today. He smelled of the ocean, clean and fresh. He was strong and enormous in size, but it was perfect. Those seconds were wonderful, I wish I could have more. It felt so right, although it was wrong.

My heart nearly beat out of my chest and I wished he had kissed me, but he was right. It could never happen. I am a married woman.

There is no future for us.

†††

September 17, 1621

What is that woman up to? Today I walked hand in hand with Rosa-Lee on the upper deck and Kayla was there. She spoke with Cisco. My Cisco, her hand on his arm. Did he welcome it? Oh, Please God. Don't let him turn out to be just another man who wants to bed me, only to run off again. I cannot take that.

Rosa-Lee wrapped herself around his leg the moment she saw him. The Captain was not pleased. I saw the fury raging in his eyes. Then I saw the pleading in Cisco's eyes before he looked away.

I removed her from him immediately, but that left him in the presence of Kayla and for some reason the woman laughed at me. I am a lady of noble birth, my upbringing beyond reproach. Am I now in contest with a slave?
For the love of a sailor.

†††

Cisco - September 18, 1621

This day started well and ended in disaster.

Qonchita found me talking to that slave girl. She merely walked up to me and started to introduce herself while she placed her hand on my arm. She looked at me as if I were her last hope.

Just then I saw the disappointment, the hurt on Qonchita's face. But I could not talk to her. To make matters worse the little girl refused to let go of me and cried when her mother took her away. Captain Breno saw everything and his eyes spat fire.

I have been warned.

†††

Qonchita - *September 19, 1621*

Today was an unpleasant day on the ship. The Captain worked Cisco almost to death. I heard the men talking. He received no water or food for the day and under the scorching sun it had to be unbearable. I wanted to offer him water at least but another sailor stopped me.

Cisco avoided me, and Rosa-Lee snivelled the entire day.

The Captain and Faro sneered down at him while they talked about me, as if I am a common whore! How could Faro do this to me? I felt so ashamed. Some of the sailors laughed at me. The man who stopped me asked me to leave the deck because I would make matters worse for Cisco. It was hard to leave him there. Tired, thirsty and blood-shed.

Rosa-Lee cried once again when I took her below and when I passed the compartment in the hull where the slaves were held Kayla laughed openly at me.

I felt betrayed at her actions.

It is all my fault. I cannot give in and make matters worse for him.

I explained to my four-year-old daughter, but I doubt she understood. She missed Cisco. That was all there was to it. But I will have to watch her.

I cannot allow him to suffer because of us.

†††

September 21, 1621

Today Alfonso, Cisco's friend, the man who stopped me when I wanted to offer him water, helped us to have a few minutes of privacy on the deck.

It was short but worth it. I simply had to see him. I had to know if he was well. The last two days the captain made him slave away while everyone snickered behind his back. How could they do this to this man?

He is a gentle, kind and a loving man. How could they treat him like that? But I had to make sure he was fine. I had to, before I would finally let go of him.
I begged him to kiss me and at first, he was hesitant. I pressed myself against him and turned my face upward, stretching as high as I could. He was so tall that even if I stood on my tiptoes I could not reach his face. For a long minute he fought it. I saw the hesitation, the fight for control, but eventually he lowered his head and we kissed for the first time. It was everything I hoped it would be. That one kiss held promises of a future we both knew was futile to hope for. But that kiss told me what he felt.

He felt the same. His breath was warm on my face as his eyes raked over mine. He did not conceal the look of love as he whispered my name. It all told me that he felt the same way.

In that few minutes we allowed ourselves the time to dream, to hope, to love.

I love him. The emotion swept me from my feet, but I was not startled about it. It was a peace that settled deep within me and I know that this is the man I have lost my heart to.

I have no remorse in loving Cisco Almaida.

†††

Cisco - September 21, 1621

It was a mistake. I shouldn't have kissed her. But how can I resist the one woman I truly love? She loves me. That was the most pleasurable wonderful thing that has ever happened to me. This lady, a woman of noble birth, loves me, an ordinary sailor man.

She was worried about me. She kept on repeating that she would do whatever she could to make my life easier. But we both know it was not to be.

Captain Breno is a stern and vicious man. He seldom listens to anyone. Nor does he take advice from a woman, even one as highborn as Qonchita.

What a beautiful name. It suits her. In my arms today, she was far from the "ice queen" others have called her.

I love her.

†††

Qonchita - *September 22, 1621*

Rosa-Lee was hard to control yesterday and with all the strength she had she fought against me to be with Cisco. I could

17

not blame her. That is where I want to be. In his arms. I can still feel them around me; still feel the touch of his lips.

When she got away from me, she ran up to him and held him as if her life depended on it. She refused to let go, even with gentle urging from him. She cried so loud that it drew everyone's attention. Captain Breno made it plain he was not impressed with her innocent display. When I finally did get her away, I pleaded for Cisco's life. I was sure the vicious man was going to do something to him. But he said he would not harm his own crew. I really hoped that was the case. But when I tried to get Cisco's attention, he refused to look at me. I am afraid for him.

Faro tried after that to console Rosa-Lee, but she was so scared of him that she sobbed and panicked to get away. He was not pleased about her open disdain towards him. He slapped her and dropped her on the deck. Every eye was on us. I felt so ashamed.

Alfonso came and helped me with her and led me to our cabin. Cisco disappeared, and Faro went back to the Captain's cabin, no doubt.

Today I heard rumours. Some of the slave girls entertained them during the night. One woman, robust and ample in her curves, sneered at me today. High and mighty, she looked down at me as if I am beneath her.

Her dress revealed everything. Her yellow teeth were a sharp contrast against her pale skin. She reeked of alcohol and tobacco, Faro's favorite vices besides women. No doubt she was one of the favorites.

How could he embarrass me like this? He has no respect for me or Rosa-Lee.

I saw Kayla again, briefly. She looked down at me and refused to speak to me. What I did to her I don't know.

†††

September 22, 1621

I cannot believe what I saw today. The captain flogged Cisco like an animal. My heart was ripped in pieces as I watched in horror, that giant of a man sprawled out against the ropes and flogged like a common criminal.

They all laughed and joked around him, and like the man I know he is, he took it silently. His skin split open as blood seeped from his wounds. He was covered in his own blood from the shoulders down. How could he endure it?

I tried to run to him, but someone held me back.

Sobs wracked through me as he arched in pain when the salt water splashed over him. He roared in agony and four men carried him away. He was limp between them. He had to be unconscious. When I wanted to go to him the captain refused my request.

How can I sit here knowing he is in pain? I must do something.

I need to find away.

I am just glad that Rosa-Lee did not witness this brutality.

My heart aches for her and for him. She searched for him all day, but I simply had no heart to tell her the truth. It would break her heart.

†††

September 23, 1621

Finally, Alfonso managed to get me to Cisco. When I reached him, he had a high fever? I brought some ointment and tended his wounds. He was delirious, calling out my name. I made him as comfortable as I could. For a long time, I sat next to him and watched as he slept. Several times I calmed him down when the fever-induced dreams made him want to get out of the bed. The moment I spoke to him and told him how much I love him he was peaceful and slept. I wanted to stay but Alfonso convinced me it would not be wise for the captain to find me there.

At least I know he will be all right tonight. Alfonso promised me he will stay close and let me know if anything changes.

I miss Cisco.

†††

September 26, 1621

Today the sea was stormy. The clouds formed over us, dark and menacing. But at least Cisco is better. He had his first meal in three days. Alfonso assured me he would be all right. I could only see him for short intervals in the last few days. Alfonso always guarded the door while I am with him.

Cisco is strong. I know that. Soon he will be up. I loved this time. I could attend to him and touch him often. I know I love him. Somehow, I will find a way to be with him always.

But I must admit the weather has me worried. Even the captain is not his usual confident self. I really hope the ship will hold up.

It took a while to get Rosa-Lee to sleep. The motion of the ship was fiercer than what we are used to. It rolls from side to side, the upper decks swaying into the waves. My stomach churns with every motion.

Oh Lord, keep us safe. Help us to find a way to be together.

1

Qonchita - *December 25, 1623*

It has been two years since our journey of survival began in Africa. Two years since I have written anything down in my diary, the only book I was able to save on that hopeless night of September 29, 1621.

But before I capture those terrible events, I want to pen down my love's reaction to the estate we will occupy for the rest of our lives.

In the end it became possible for us to be together. The price was high, but we have survived, and I know with Cisco at my side I can face anything else.

As a Christmas gift I gave him full ownership of my estate. It has been handed down from generation to generation of Artiagas. *I knew he would be the perfect land owner to continue the legacy my family started, and that Rosa-Lee's inheritance was safe.*

When Rosa-Lee climbed on his lap to give him a big wet kiss he smiled down at her and gave her a bear hug. The last few days he had been extremely emotional. We both felt a deep compassion for him. I feel proud to know this man, my husband, Cisco Almaida. When I handed him the papers, he was shocked? Disbelief shone clear in the blue depths of his eyes. He had the same expression when we first arrived two days ago.

He could not believe the sight of the large estate or the castle, built by my great-great grandfather all those years ago.

When we arrived Cisco only stared at the estate, the manicured gardens and lawns only yellow due to the cold weather, and I had to encourage him to step into the castle as man of the house. This was more than he ever dreamt of. His mind was stunned at the magnitude of the riches he faced.

I had told him about the place before, to prepare him, but I knew he would only appreciate it fully once he saw it.

He stood in the enormous foyer of the castle and gaped in awe. The magnificent wooden staircase spiralled to the upper levels. The black and white marble tiles gleamed in the late sunlight. Fires were already laid all through the house, for which we were grateful. The staff had done a magnificent work in maintaining the place while we were gone.

He felt overwhelmed by it all until Rosa-Lee reached for his hand and walked with him to the parlour with its exquisite furniture, tapestries and golden framed paintings of past generations. She chattered non-stop, even if it was her first visit. But the difference was, she is used to these riches and he was not.

After we settled in, he walked the estate literally for the next two days, and I accompanied him. The land was surrounded with a rapid-flowing river with tree lines on both sides, the castle looked impressive, built out of stone and brick, standing three stories tall in the Portugal sun. Fields ready for the next season.

The castle itself was filled with generations worth of treasures; heavy hand-crafted furniture, art, and family portraits, tapestries bought in India, China, Spain and Africa, rich in colour, hung on the walls of each room.

At first, he could not comprehend the papers, or his new title as land owner. He struggled for words this morning but once it was clear that I was serious he accepted the responsibilities as property owner. This was a difficult time for Portugal. The country was in a transitional phase and landowners were often unfair dictators. But I knew he was wise and would treat his people with respect and kindness. He would give them what was fair, distributing our wealth for the benefit of all.

Cisco is willing to learn. His good, kind heart draws people closer. Already he and Franco, the manager of the estate, have a close friendship. His first lesson was to learn to ride his horse, another present from Rosa-Lee. She was so excited when the horse was presented to him that she giggled with pure joy when the animal was brought out. His face lit up in childlike wonder at the powerfully-muscled black stallion. When he approached the animal, the horse responded in like fashion. It took us a while to get him back in the house.

What a delight the day has been. Alfonso will leave soon on the ship Cisco received from the D.E.I.C. for his brave efforts during the last two years. Kayla and Derek will leave for their new home in Spain and the house will become ours alone. There are so many things I still want to show him. I can hardly wait.

But tonight, I will give him his greatest gift when I reveal my pregnancy to him. I just know this will leave him speechless.

†††

It was the year 1641 on the south coast of Portugal. The lone figure of a young woman looked over the vast blue sea. A breeze rippled playfully on the water's surface. To her it spelt trouble, haunting her thoughts with *what if's,* reliving the past as if it were just yesterday, crystal clear in her mind. Every day for the last two weeks she had looked at the horizon, hoping to see her father's well-known merchant ship with his ensign flag appear. But there was no sign. The foreboding feelings accumulated again within her heart, making her anxious and troubled.

While she waited, she read her parents' diaries, a present for her eighteenth birthday, and her most treasured possession in the whole world, for the umpteenth time. The leather-bound books were soft under her touch, the papers already yellowing. She had read them so often that she knew them by heart, but still they evoked in her a sense of belonging. They held her past but also her future. At twenty-four she knew her future would be colourful and beautiful. She felt safe when reading the pages, and knew if they had made it, she would make it as well.

Coming on the ship was her eagerly-awaited younger brother, only sixteen years of age. He had been so excited about his first voyage as a sailor that they could hardly stay in the same house with him. Their father had taught them all about the sea since they could understand and walk.

He had taught them to read the stars at night, to read charts, navigating their own way. He sent them on the ship for countless lessons; lessons they never tired of.

Pedro always had a bigger love for the sea. He was more like their father in his kind-heartedness and was a gentle giant with dark blond hair. He was more excited about the lifestyle of a sailor, exploring new countries, loving the openness of the seas. Their father told the stories of his adventures and especially the time she, Rosa-Lee, and their mother had met him. He was still a sailor then, and the tale included the two years it took them to get back to Portugal after leaving India, where their journey had begun, and Rosa-Lee had been born.

As a birthday gift, her father had given Pedro the position of cabin boy to Captain Alfonso, his good friend, to go out to India. He went away for seven months, and by her father's calculations, he should have already been back.

Her other brother, Manuel was the farmer. He inherited the love of the land and its people from his mother. He also looked like their father in build, but his skin and hair were darker, like Rosa-Lee's and her mother's. Manuel had a mild and caring heart that made him loveable and accessible to the villagers.

At the tender age of eighteen, he was already a leader. The people looked up to him, and along with their father, he built up the estate and expanded the business.

Rosa-Lee knew that this delay in Pedro's safe return was hard on her mother and father. Not knowing his whereabouts was difficult but they could only remain calm, waiting. The mood tensed in their home as her father paced the passageways of the castle, anxious and nervous.

Finally, on Sunday afternoon of the second week, Rosa-Lee saw sails heading their way. Shading her eyes, she squinted as she watched the sails coming nearer to the shore at a tormenting slow rate. Rosa-Lee could now see that it was the *Contra O*

Vento. The smaller frigate usually accompanied the merchant ship as extra security. It was faster and streamlined, not her father's bulky merchant ship.

Dread filled her heart as she watched the sailors running around on the deck, furling the sails to dock in the harbour. The ensign on the top of the main mast certainly was her father's crest. Cisco Almaida was a merchant working for the D.E.I.C. He received his first ship eighteen years ago after serving at the sea for nineteen years as a sailor. It was a reward for his bravery and leadership during that fatal voyage where her biological father had passed away along with two hundred and sixty-four crew members, slaves and passengers.

Gathering the cream fabric of her skirt in her hands she ran down the road to the harbour to meet the captain of the ship she recognized. She was hoping that it would be good news about her brother, but the sense of dread did not leave her small body as her chestnut hair streamed behind her, her small oval face wary and troubled.

The months of waiting in anticipation of Pedro had been too long. They stayed a close-knit family, especially Mother, Father and herself, but the two boys who had not yet had adventures did not understand the dangerous side of a sailing ship. It sounded foreign and distant to them, just stories they had heard all their lives. But Rosa-Lee and her parents knew how quickly things could change on the sea. They had lived through it and had survived its worst.

Pedro was still very young, inexperienced about life.

Rosa-Lee's dress whipped against her legs as she ran down the shoreline into the town, her lungs burning with the unusual exercise. Today she did not see the splendour of the sea or land, the birds flying just over the top of her head. She did not notice the familiar faces, townspeople who waved at her and flashed toothy smiles. With only the *Contra O Vento* coming in she was worried.

When she reached the berth, the captain stood on the bridge at the side, peering through the tackle works, deep in thought. As the plank lowered onto the pier, she had a sinking feeling that something was very wrong; that life as she knew it is about to change.

"Captain, any news?" she shouted.

Visible sorrow marked the older man's tanned face along with tired lines from hard days on the sea.

"Yes child, I have news, but it is not good news, I am afraid." With short, uneven steps he descended the plank. His normally immaculate dress was crinkled and filthy; a grey, unkept beard shadowed his thin cheek bones.

As he reached her, he swallowed, avoiding her at first, and then reached for her hands, his voice filled with sorrow.

"You will have to be very strong for your parents." He patted her hands as if to comfort her. "This news is not good. Come, let us go to them. I will speak to all of you." Panic gripped Rosa-Lee's heart.

What can be so terrible? She looked up at him. Captain Jean le Blanc was around her father's age with dark blue eyes and black hair, grey visible all around his head. Normally he was a very proud man, shoulders straight, his voice strong as a captain's

28

should be. Now he walked as if he were in pain, sounding out of breath and speaking as if it gave him great pain to talk. Looping her hand in his arm, she walked next to him, supporting him. She tried to convince him to talk to her, to find out more detail but he was silent all the way.

As they walked away, dark ochre eyes framed in thick black lashes followed them with a curious fixation on the chestnut-coloured head of the young woman and the bodice of the cream dress clinging to her body, outlining it perfectly. The owner of the eyes squinted the left one as he framed the small waist in the air with his fingers, and thought, *Perfect.*

Jumping down off a barrel in one swift motion, he followed them at a slow pace. Staying in the shadows, he pulled his black hat low over his eyes and wrapped a heavy black cloak around his lean body to conceal any identifying features of his clothing. His silver sword sheathed alongside his narrow hip thudded against a knee-height black boot.

†††

As they walked to the castle Captain Jean's pace was slow, as if he had to think about each step he took, and he still sounded out of breath.

"Are you well, Captain?" Concerned, Rosa-Lee's dark brown eyes rested on him.

"Yes, dear, I will be fine once we reach your father's house." He gave her a sloppy smile.

"Can't I get the carriage? It will be more comfortable."

29

"No, dear, we are almost there. I am used to hardships. Don't worry about me." Patting her hand as she held onto him, the captain looked ghastly.

As they reached the castle, he hesitated to go through the heavy doors but continued, sweat pearling on his forehead, weaker from the walk, breathless and pale.

Finally, standing before her father, he handed him a letter. With shaking hands, he said,

"Cisco, my dear friend." He clipped every word, taking a breath between each. "I don't know how to give this news to you." Shame filled his countenance as Rosa-Lee squeezed his hand, and his smile at her was grim.

"I feel I have failed you, not only as a friend, but as an employee."

Cisco reached out to his friend, troubled sombreness on his face, taking the letter, first looking at the white, folded sheet, then back at his friend.

"Jean what is going on? Are you in pain? Come, sit down, my friend."

As her father helped Captain Jean sit down Rosa-Lee saw that blood seeped beneath his jacket from his upper leg and dripped onto the tiled floor.

"Father! The captain is wounded, look!" she cried out in distress, kneeling in front of him and spreading the jacket. His black pants were stained with blood, the metallic scent filling their noses.

Cisco put the letter down and reached him in one stride. He crouched next to Rosa-Lee, his towering body warm and reassuring and his voice steady.

"Let me look at that leg." his piercing eyes dropped first to his friend's leg then stared up at him.

"What has happened to you, Jean?"

"It is a long story, my friend. I don't know if I will be able to tell you. It hurts me too much. I have failed you, you and your family."

"How did you fail me, Jean? You don't make any sense. Calm down and tell us what is going on. Is it about Pedro? And where is Alfonso?"

"Yes, it is Pedro, and I hope he is still alive. When I left him at the Isle of Saint Marie, he was barely alive. Alfonso died trying to defend Pedro from being captured by the pirates."

They could hear the sharp intake of breath as Qonchita walked in. They all paled.

"What about Pedro and pirates?" She looked at Cisco, panic filling her dark brown eyes. "Cisco, what is going on?"

She looked at her husband and then at Jean, who was very pale, drops of blood forming a pool at his booted foot.

"Rosa-Lee, please send for the doctor at once, dear," said Qonchita. She stayed calm as she knelt before their friend.

"Yes, mother." Rosa-Lee rushed out the door and straight into the arms of Franco, their horse-handler.

"Franco, we need the doctor here at once! Please get him. There is no time to waste!"

"Yes, ma'am!" Franco's stallion stood nearby grazing. He was a dark brown colour with long legs, extremely fast, his muscles well defined, rippling under his shiny coat. When Franco called his name, his ears perked to full attention. With a whinny he was ready for action. Franco pulled himself-into the saddle with one hand. Horse and man moved as one as they race down the gravel road, dust swirling around them.

Rosa-Lee returned to the living room where her mother and father still stood at Captain Jean's chair. He was even paler than before, and her parents looked worried. Her mother held a cloth on the leg, trying to stop the bleeding, pale with worry.

Her father held the letter with shaking hands and as she stepped closer, his right arm fell to his side. The letter, open in his hand, shook as a grey pallour covered his face.

"Father, what is wrong?"

Her father did not say anything; her mother covered her face in her hands, sobbing. The cloth fell on the floor and a dark stain formed, unnoticed. Rosa-Lee removed the letter still clutched in her father's big hand and began to read. The more she read, the angrier she got.

Cisco Almaida

It is a shame that we must meet under these circumstances, for I have heard about your bravery over the years; but a man must make a living. Consider this a business transaction.

I have your youngest son, Pedro, in my custody at the Isle of Saint Marie. He assured me that you are a wealthy man and can pay me a healthy ransom for his release.

For your son's release I demand 2000 in gold coins by the end of four months or he will be dead. It will all depend on how quickly you can deliver.

He talked about his lovely sister so often. Let her bring it. I can use some feminine company.

Do not try anything. I did send my second-in-command with your Captain Jean to watch over all the proceedings and to make sure Rosa-Lee comes along.

His life is in your hands.

The Falcon

"How dare he?" She lifted the paper in the air, perplexed, angry, and bitter at this unknown Falcon. As her hand dropped, still trembling, she looked at her parents with blazing eyes. She had to read the letter twice to understand the contents. The more she read, the angrier she grew.

"How dare he?" she spat out.

"You have to leave tomorrow morning early. Otherwise you will not make the deadline," Captain Jean gasped. "His second-in-command is his son, a ruthless and cunning man. It was he who wounded me before I got off the ship, to make sure I would deliver the message."

"What is his name?" Rosa-Lee asked, still seething.

"Roberto. He is very sly and very dangerous. I would do as they say if I were in your shoes," he said through clenched teeth.

Finally, Cisco spoke, and the anger in his voice was unmistakable.

"Who does this man think he is, to command in this manner money, my daughter and my son's life, all in one breath?"

"My father is used to getting what he wants, and this is a small price to pay for your son's life, I would say." A very tall, dark-haired man, the expression on his face determined and fierce, stood in the doorway, filling it with his large frame. They had not noticed him before and swung toward the deep baritone voice. A scar ran from the corner of his left lip to his left eye. The deep ochre shade of those eyes made him look even more dangerous.

He wore black trousers with high boots. A white shirt showed beneath his long black jacket. In his large hand that looked like a claw to Rosa-Lee he nonchalantly held a black hat. He glared straight into her father's own piercing eyes without any faltering of his gaze.

She clenched her hands in fists, eyes blazing at the black cloaked man, the smirk on his face clearly in defiance of any law.

"We leave tomorrow morning at six. Be there or bear the consequences." His eyes shifted to her with amusement and with a mockingly courteous nod to her, he turned and left. They were all stunned in disbelief.

"How dare you?" She shouted at his back.

He turned, glancing back at her, appraising her as if she were the most despicable thing he had ever seen. The guffaw that burst from his throat rolled over her. She stamped her foot in frustration on the marble floor.
Though his voice was cold and distant, his eyes were fiery darts pinning her to attention to him. "Be warned, *Môn Petite,* that you do not wake the beast." And he left her standing there. For a moment, fear gripped her heart and her knees buckled. She melted into the love seat.

Her dress billowed around her in an unlady-like fashion. She was crestfallen at the very idea that she would be in this cold man's presence for the next four months. But she would go.

†††

December 26, 1623

Cisco Almaida, land owner. Words I never thought would stand together. But after yesterday it was true. I am a land owner, married to the most beautiful woman in the world. And soon to be a father. My heart wants to beat out of my chest.

A father. The greatest gift of all. When Qonchita revealed it to me last night I was, to say the least, speechless. I cried for the first time in my life. I cried. I had nothing else to say and I wrapped her in my arms and held her all night. She has blessed me since the moment she stepped in my life. She has made me have pride in myself. Because of her I can fulfil my dreams.

God, Your Word is true. You bless the pure in heart. You knew my desires and You fulfilled them. Even when I walked through the valley of death and feared, you remained faithful. How awesome is Your Grace?

Help me to stay true to Your Word, true to my new title, and to use it for good. Help me to be a husband and father as you have ordained from the foundation of the world.

I praise your Holy Name.

Amen

2

January 2, 1624

We spent our first Christmas and New Year together as a family. Cisco was like a child, riding his horse all over the place. There was never a dull moment with him around. Rosa-Lee is blossoming with him as her father. Her giggles of delight fill the castle's passageways and the staff is happier than I can remember.

This is all thanks to Cisco.

Cisco, the man who always steps up when the situation calls for it. He was the one who acted when the ship was splitting into pieces on that fateful day when our lives changed forever. He took charge of a panic-filled crew, all the while his back was still healing. When the crew started to drink all the whiskey to soften the blow of death, he kept calm. When slaves drowned in the whiskey in their attempts to get there first, he kept us safe.

He made a harness for Rosa-Lee and me on that fateful day when eighty-nine people died during the ship's demise. He simply put me on his back and Rosa-Lee on his chest and jumped into the swells of the foaming sea. He swam to the shore where he made sure we were safe before he helped anyone else. Of course, once Captain Breno was on land he took it out on Cisco. Jealous because he did not save everyone, and the people admired Cisco.

Those first days on the beach, stranded on the East Coast of Africa were terrifying. But that was only the start of our journey.

Cisco built us a hut to shelter us from the continuous rains. He was the one that made sure there was food enough for everyone. The people trusted him more and for that he was punished again. Again, flogged like an animal when he shot a deer to feed the many mouths.

But we would have died if not for him.

He saved me when Faro wanted to rape me. He saved Rosa-Lee when a lion wanted to kill her. He never complained; he did what was necessary and everyone benefited from it, including my husband and the captain. Those days were filled with horrific scenes of death and survival. They would always stay in my mind.

†††

"Cisco, you have called for me. Where's the patient?"

Cisco Almaida visibly shook for the first time in his life. His whole family was endangered by one man's insanity. Wrapping his arms around his wife, he caressed her back and in return, tiny hands held his broad back, caressing him.

Watching his daughter over on the settee, he could see raw emotions running over the youthful face. Then at last he followed the familiar voice to his friend and family doctor. He swallowed at the bile in his throat, got his voice back, and said,

"Doctor Vasco, please come in. It is Jean. He was wounded." Cisco turned to Captain Jean, still holding his wife around the shoulders. The captain was still sitting on the chair, as white as a sheet, miserably in pain.

38

"Is there somewhere we could lie him down so that he can be more comfortable?"

"Yes, Doctor, please follow me," said Rosa-Lee, who had come to her senses, lifting her eyes and wiping the tears away. Her mother was still distracted. She did not hear anything else around her. Tears streamed down her face, but she made no sound.

Straightening herself, Rosa-Lee walked to the injured Captain Jean, helping him to his feet. With the aid of the doctor, supporting him between them, she got him to the nearest bedroom, where they laid him down. Rosa-Lee helped to remove his jacket. They saw the gaping sword-wound clearly, his shirt and trousers on the right side drenched with blood.

"I will go get some warm water, Doctor. Please excuse me."

"Thanks, Rosa-Lee." She walked out, the anger she felt earlier was building inside of her. *Who do these people think they are, this pirate Roberto, son of the Falcon, using Pedro and myself shamelessly, and wounding our friend in this manner?*

I will go, but if they think that I will stay as their female companion, they have another thing coming! She sneered unwomanly.

I will show them! She was filled with outrage.

She knew how to defend herself. Her father had taught her the skill of the pistol and the sword. *I will give them hell. For now, I will play along. But the moment I get an opportunity, I will take revenge for this blatant arrogance.*

Her hazel eyes spat fire and with a very fierce posture, she walked to the kitchen to get the warm water and then speak to her father. They had to know that they could count on her to bring Pedro back.

†††

"Mother, Father, please let me go. I will bring Pedro back safely." Her father had refused to give in to the demands of the pirate.

"I will not send my only daughter to that place. I have heard many things about this pirate and Isle of Saint Marie. I will go and get him!" Cisco raised his voice in frustration and anger.

"But Father, the letter states plainly that I must go. We must do as they say, else they will kill Pedro."

They argued for a long time about this. Even Manuel said he would go, but his father just looked at him with a glare and refused. He had to tend to the farm.

Finally, when it was already late that evening, her Father reluctantly gave in. Mother walked up to him and wrapped her arms around his waist, pleading and crying, but they all knew there was nothing they could do. They had to give in to the demands of the pirate or lose their son. However, the thought of their daughter in the hands of those brutes terrified them.

Cisco knew what they did to women, how they treated them. Rosa-Lee was as good as dead once she was there.

How would they live with themselves?

"Please, Father, you have taught me all you know, and I can defend myself. Don't worry, please, I will be fine."

"Trust that what you have taught me will save me and Pedro." Her eyes were wide with determination as she stepped closer to them. Cisco gathered her closer, her face pressed into his shoulder. He held her for a very long time, shaking.

Her mother rubbed her back and said, "We love you, dear, please come back safely."

"Yes, mama." She kissed Qonchita's soft cheek, still beautiful after all these years, her back rigid as she composed herself.

"I will let you go, Rosa, but you need to let me know as soon as possible what is going on so that I know if I have to come looking for you," Cisco said gruffly.

"Yes, Father." standing on her tip toes, she kissed his handsome face. "I need to pack still, and it is late."

"Yes, dear, I will bring the coins to you in a moment." He hugged her once more before he let her go. Mother and father stood at the door for a while and she could hear him mutter something to her and Manuel, who walked away, angry at the whole situation. This was not the time to be a hero.

As Rosa-Lee packed her trunks with her earthly belongings Qonchita came to sit with her. Qonchita's eyes were moist but she was obviously more under control while she sat and watched. She handed her daughter petticoats to pack in and only sniffed few times. This was hard on Rosa-Lee. She knew how her mother had struggled to forget the turmoil of their time in Africa, the nights she woke terrified of the horrors they had seen. Rosa-Lee really hoped that this would not cause those nightmares to return.

Because she was only four during those times, they had sheltered her from the worst parts of it. She did not experience half the nightmares Mama did. Papa was the strong one who kept them sane during those times, making a new future for them all.

He was the pillar and he would be the pillar as always, her giant Papa. He was the man she started to know as a friend and who had become her father. She hardly remembered her biological father. The abuse they had suffered under him had made him easy to forget.

"Mama, please, don't make it difficult. I will be fine. You and Papa have taught me everything you know. I will be all right. Just believe in me, please."

"I do believe in you, Rosa-Lee, but still, this is very dangerous. The outcome can be devastating for both you and Pedro."

"I have a few plans up my sleeve for this Falcon and his son, Mother. Please calm down." She said with much conviction.

Her mother looked at her in shock, grabbing her shoulders. "Rosa-Lee! You will not try something foolish and get yourself killed. Promise me."

"No, mother." She held her mother's hands, kissing them. "I will be back with Pedro, I promise."

She hid her pistol and knife in her trunk. *This pirate will not have me on a platter; Rosa-Lee Almaida is made of pure Almaida blood, tough enough to face anything.*

Later Rosa-Lee lay in her bed, eyes wide open. She had to swallow hard as the enormity of what she was about to face occurred to her and tears ran down her cheeks. She allowed them to run freely.

Come tomorrow morning, fear would be the last emotion she had the luxury of giving into. Her life would depend on her skill and alertness.

†††

January 4, 1624

Last night I was awakened by Qonchita once again. She panicked and moaned uncontrollably in her sleep. It took me awhile to calm her enough for her to realize we were safe.

The turmoil of our journey plagued her. Last night she dreamt we were back on the beach where Kayla tried to seduce me. The slave girl had pretended to sleep with me so that Qonchita would desert me. The mere fact that Qonchita did not speak to me for a few days almost killed me.

Because of her I had the courage to do what I did to get us out of that place. Faro's attempt to rape her terrified her. I wish I could take those haunting images away. Every time after such an ordeal she melted into my arms, looking forlorn and lost. My heart ached for her and for what we were going through.

The image of her feet, skin worn away to a bloody pulp from walking, her slippers torn, is engraved in me. Those first days were terrible, when we realized help was not coming and we would have to walk. People fell from exhaustion because the captain refused to stop. The lack of food and the constant rain stalled us over and over. I still hear the screams as wild animals captured people and dragged them into the bushes. I carried Qonchita for days through that brush with Rosa-Lee on my back. Faro never attempted to help them. Not that I would have let him.

The man was more interested in the slave girls that travelled with us. There were times that I had to bite my tongue when I caught him in the act. The man was simply arrogant in his dealings, but those women loved him.

Those days were hard on my lady. But she never complained. She took everything with her head held high, a true lady to the bone.

I swore to myself that I would keep her safe, protect her. I did not care what any one said, her safety came first. Those days when I carried her, I knew without any doubt that I loved her, but I never revealed it, although I wanted to. That kiss was the only one we ever dared to share, so I kept my distance as much as I could.

It was hard to watch her, yet she had this strength in her that made her to stand up and go on, no matter what.

Now, to have her in my arms every night is a blessing. I can kiss her all I want. I make love to her and she simply melts in my arms.

She is my joy, my delight. I will love her always.

3

January 15, 1624

Today was an exceptionally cold day and we spent it indoors. I love days like this where we can sit around the hearth and read, talk and enjoy each other's company. Rosa-Lee was on top of Cisco most of the time. She loves her daddy so much. Her laughter fills the castle. I can hardly wait for this little one to come. My protruding tummy is a joy for Cisco. He simply cannot keep his hands off me.

Today I think back to the many days and weeks we walked through the grassy plains of Africa. I remember the exhaustion, the heat, and the insects that bit us day and night. Then in the afternoons the rains would drench us completely so that the nights were miserable. We faced hunger for days on end because Captain Breno refused to let us rest and get the required food. I learned to eat anything in my walk, from tree bark to grass and leaves. Anything would do just to get the hunger pains under control.

There were days that I did not know how we got at a certain point. My body and soul were so tired for lack of anything basic.

After two months of aimless walks we finally arrived in an empty stad, *a town. No one was there and as we searched the empty huts in the hope of food, we were once again faced with no relieve of our hunger cramps. A lonely dog barked, seeking attention from the Captain. He shot it.*

People scrambled to get to it first. In disgust I watched as they ate it just like that.

Someone found rotten maize. Again, people ate it and got stomach convulsions. Two people died afterwards.

The one thing that would always remain in my thoughts was the face of the pregnant woman we found shot dead by our captain and left to bleed to death. He was a cruel man. He wanted to punish me when I hit him out of pure rage after the death of that young woman. Her death was senseless.

Cisco thought it wise to take me away. In the process we were attacked by savages. We ran, Rosa-Lee in Cisco's arms, me right behind him and Kayla, who was never far behind, followed us. In the confusion we were separated from the group. Two days later when we found them, we were charged with mutiny. It was the first time I saw Cisco completely lose his temper.

He is a big man, taller and bulkier than most. He towered over Captain Breno and for the first time I saw fear in the Captain's eyes.

Cisco was captured by some of the Captain's followers, but the rest of the group attacked them and eventually they let go of him. From that day forward the Captain was less hostile toward Cisco.

Those were trying times. Our endurance was pushed to the limit.

†††

Commotion filled the harbour early the next morning. The sun tinted the sky in an orange-gold, a few featherlike clouds floating in the heavens.

Captains barked out commands to their scurrying crews. Sailors raced around to get all the cargo onto the ships, walking the plank in swift long strides laden with luggage, crates or chicken pens. While men scaled the tackle works, hollering to each other, a few already swabbed the decks with Holystone and salt water, whistling a cheerful tune.

The whole place looked alive and festive. However, festivity was the last thing in the hearts of the Almaida family. With sombre faces, they watched sailors carry Rosa-Lee's trunks up the plank of the *Contra O Vento*. The small, streamlined frigate lay waiting in the calm water.

Cisco and Qonchita stood next to Manuel, who watched the activities with interest. Rosa-Lee knew his heart was not with the sea. This was his life, here, working the land. She would miss him, her big bear of a brother.

She bravely smiled at her family and they held her for a moment in silence. They had said all they could. Now they all had to believe that this voyage would not end in disaster.

Rosa-Lee was just hugging her mother when they heard a stern, brisk voice behind them.

"Very touching, but it is time."

Rosa-Lee saw the pirate looking at her from the ship, the same amusement from the previous evening in his eyes. He looked menacing, unwavering in the same dark clothes of the previous day. She met his gaze in the same manner; unwavering, defiant. His chuckle sent fury into her eyes.

Roberto saw the fury and it drew him. *This will be an interesting time with her aboard the ship. The Falcon is going to know her, but there is no harm in having some fun.*

Ochre eyes roamed over the enticing body wrapped in green taffeta. The dark braided hair lay over a creamy shoulder. Her bodice clung to the small frame in the latest fashion. Her perky breasts looked ripe for the plucking. He grinned at the picture he knew he will enjoy.

She stepped away from her parents with anger still visible on her face. She gathered her dress in her hands and walked up the plank with a steady gait and a rigid back, small shoulders straight, showing no fear, to where the pirate waited. She looked at him, eyes locking his with defiance. His guffaw rumbled up his throat, mocking her. She pulled her chin up. Without a word, she turned to wave to her parents.

Rosa-Lee Almaida has some backbone, Roberto smiled. *Backbone I would like to break and bend to my will. Yes, I am going to enjoy this voyage.*

He turned his attention back to the ship and barked orders still aware of Rosa-Lee at the railing.

She stood there until the white sails were set high above her, the breeze filling them with snapping sounds. Wood creaking, the ship started to sail away from the harbour. They moved further and further over the blue depths, small waves tossing against the hull, until she could not see her parents any more.

Refusing to give in to the emotions which swept over her, she finally turned away from the rail. Two men stood with buckets filled with sea water and splashed it over the wooden deck.

Some were up in the tackle of the sails, the watchman in his crow's nest.

Many of them watched her with curiosity, toothy grins on their faces, talking to one another. Some of them looked at her like a morsel they could sample as dark, lustful eyes followed her.

The captain stood on the bridge next to the boatswain looking down at her with his mock expression, an expression she intended to have the pleasure of wiping from his face. The man on his right-hand side was rather good looking, with a smile on his handsome face. His eyes followed her, and he gave her a light nod. She nodded back in greeting, which caused Roberto to frown, looking at his second in command with a stern gaze. He muttered something, and the man looked away with a smirk.

Looking around, she wondered where she would be sleeping when she heard a young male voice next to her.

"Señorita Almaida, I will show you to your sleeping quarters." His voice was pleasant to her ear and she smiled, glad to finally see a friendly face.

"I will be your chamber boy for the duration of the trip. Please follow me."

He could not be more than sixteen years old, very small in posture. Big brown eyes and had an easy smile in them. He was quite likeable, considering the predicament she was in.

Well, I am here now. I might just as well make the best of it. When she looked up, her father's flag, their family crest, had been replaced with a black pirate flag and a purple flag with a falcon underneath it. She sneered in a most unladylike way at them and followed the young man.

"What is your name?" she asked as her eyes swept over the ship, refusing to look at the defiant man on the bridge.

"I am Enrico, Señorita."

"Well, Enrico, show me the way."

He took her below deck to the stern of the ship to a large cabin with rich, purple velvet curtains and bed drapes. Surprised at the richness she looked around and took in the sparse furniture. She expected a bunk but finding a bed in there was so much better. A small dresser and table stood in the one corner with a chair next to it, next to the port.

"This will be your cabin, Señorita. If there is anything you need, you can pull this cord and I will be here to assist." He showed her a golden cord which hanged in the corner of the bed.

"That door leads to my cabin." He pointed out a door in the left corner of the cabin. "Breakfast will be served in your cabin, but all other meals will be eaten with the captain."

"I refuse to eat with that man. I will stay here. Please go!" Immediately she raised her voice in anger. *Who does this man think she is? I do not want any contact with him in anyway. The nerve of this man.*

Enrico nodded his head in understanding and walked out, closing the door behind him.

She unpacked her trunk into the small cupboard provided for her dresses and left a few things in the trunk for later use, especially the pistol, well-hidden for now. She realized she needed a place to put them and, looked around her room a second time.

Her room was comfortable but small; not what she enjoyed at home, but for now it suited her purposes. She found her way around easily and decided to put her knife near her bed between the folds of the curtains. It would be close enough to get to easily.

In the one corner near the window was a small tub for her bath, a luxury on a ship. Although the ship belonged to her father she had never been on it, only the larger merchant one, but her father undoubtedly thought of everything when he purchased it a few years back. Not suitable for a woman, but for this voyage it would do fine.

She was busy brushing her long hair when she heard a knock. Thinking that it will be Enrico, she answered, "Please come in."

"Señorita Almaida." The familiar stern voice greeted her. When she turned around, Roberto stood behind her. He was closer to her now than at any time since they had met, hovering over her, the menacing looks plainer to see on his face. The scar running from his left eye to the corner of his mouth made him look fierce.

"I have been informed that you will not join me for the meals, Señorita. Can I ask why not?" His voice cold, while his eyes took in the interior of the cabin.

"I will not eat with you, a pirate." Defiance was in her own cold voice. "I don't want to discuss this any further. Please leave my room." She turned away from him, peering out the porthole to the open sea, and continued brushing her hair.

She did not see the amused look that was followed by a stern one as he spoke "It is not a matter of what you want, Señorita. You will sit at my table and that is final!"

"Make me," she said through clenched teeth.

"All right, if this is how you want to play it, I am fine with that. Good day." He nodded but she did not bother to turn around to notice.

When he left, she let out her breath. She had not even realized that she was holding it. *This man will learn that I am not very willing or easy to please. I will give him hell!* She braided her long hair with trembling fingers.

The day went on without any further disturbances and she kept herself busy with needlework, sitting near the port for extra light, but for some reason she did not see Enrico again. By late afternoon, she finally decided to call for him and pulled the cord. Her throat was dry, and she was hungry. She had not eaten last night after the news they had received. This morning she was already gone before breakfast was served.

A few minutes later Enrico entered her room.

"Where is my food? I had nothing to drink or eat for the whole day," she asked, annoyed, forgetting her manners.

"I received strict instruction that no food or drink may be delivered to you, Señorita."

"Well I never!" and she bald her fist in frustration. She sneaked a look at the young man, and she wondered for a moment if her attitude would not bite her, after all she didn't know this man and four months without food would be devasting for her. Could she afford to go that route? Would the captain really force her hand like this?

"Can I at least have water?" she asked demurely, she needed time to think this through.

"No," came the abrupt reply yet he blushed. Clearly not comfortable with the position he was in.

"That conceited man. How dare he?" she cried, frustrated.

"He is the captain. When he speaks, we listen, Señorita."

"Is that right?" she asked in a sarcastic tone. "Where is he?"

"In his quarters, eating, Señorita."

"Take me to him," she demanded.

"Follow me, Señorita." Enrico kept his eyes cast down, not meeting her angry stare.

The captain's cabin lay two doors down the passageway. When she walked in, he sat lazily at his table eating a peach, his stern eyes looking straight at her as if he had expected her.

"I understand from my chamber boy that I will not be served any meals?"

"That is correct. Did you change your mind?"

"No, but it is inhumane. How dare you not give me anything? Not even water?"

"Because I am the captain, and this is my ship," He said nonchalantly and placed a slice of fruit in his mouth.

For a moment she was at a loss for words, her fists white as she clenched them. She could physically harm him by now.

"I must point out that this is my father's ship, Señor, and not yours."

"Point taken, but I am the captain, therefore my rules."

"You are a bastard!" She stamped out of the room, the fabric of her dress rustling with her anger.

†††

"How long do you think she will hold out?" Pierre, his second-in-command, asked.

"Don't know, but it will be interesting to see." Roberto placed another piece of the juicy fruit in his mouth, eating it slowly, while a smile appeared on the normally stern face.

"She has a lot of spunk," Pierre continued with a lopsided grin.

"Yes. She is a real wildcat. It will be interesting to tame her. I have all the time in the world. She will come around and see that in this world there is only one law that counts. That is mine."

Pegging the knife in his table, he stood straight, cleaning his hand. He took the last sip of his red wine before he went back to the upper deck.

Roberto liked what he saw. When Pedro told him about her, he was intrigued about the family's story, but especially about her. When the opportunity came to bring her back as a ransom price, he jumped at the chance.

It did not take much convincing to sway the Falcon so that Roberto could go and ensure that Cisco met the demands for the ransom. The Falcon knew he could trust Roberto with her. Now he had a chance to get to know her better, and maybe convince the Falcon that she would be more suitable for him. She was a stunning woman with a lot of fire in her veins, a fire that Roberto would like to ignite in ways other than anger.

By my calculation, there must be a fifteen-year's difference in our ages. I can tame her to fit into my needs quite nicely. My first impressions of her were correct.

Yes, she will do perfectly for all the plans I have for her. Yes, that anger and fury in her I am going to turn in to passion, a task that I am looking forward to in the coming months. In the, end she will be mine without a question.

For now, he decided to keep his plans to himself, to go with whatever she was planning, and then take it from there. He understood from Pedro that she was skilled with the sword and a good markswoman. Moreover, if Pedro's good marksmanship was any indication, she would be a force to be reckoned with. He would have to test her during the time they had on the open seas. *These will be an interesting four months' voyage for sure!*

Roberto chuckled to himself.

Pierre wondered what the smile was all about. He knew his friend. The man is wild among the women, usually, taking what he wants. But with this one, he acts differently, toying with her like a lion with a rabbit. Something about little Pedro's sister is of interest to the captain. It just may be the man has met his match with this young woman. Her eyes show how she feels, and she is not afraid like most. No, this one is defiant, a real wild cat, as Roberto says.

That Roberto was up to something was very clear to him. Yes, this will be an interesting time, with the stunning woman on board.

†††

January 25, 1624

I cannot believe I am already a month on the estate. A month of surprises, new opportunities and new experiences. Franco is patient with all my one hundred questions, answering them as we go along. The villagers are really an interesting lot, and already I have made a few friends.

Rosa-Lee is a constant chatterbox, which makes me smile with pleasure. What a wonderful, brilliant child. She is everything I want in a daughter. Inquisitive. Energetic. Beautiful.

And my dear wife -- how can I describe the love I feel for her? She is everything I want, need and more. My heart still jumps when she enters a room, still taking my breath away. Her raven hair still mesmerizes me, and I love to run my fingers through the silky softness.

She is brilliant, stunning and she is all mine.

Every hardship I had to endure was worth it. Every day that I spend with her is a day that I am blessed, and I cannot thank God enough for this, and for keeping us safe.

He removed every obstacle, every scoffer, and made me victorious. Through all our trials He kept us healthy when people died around us like flies. Hunger, heat, rain, sickness were daily constants in our lives, but through all that we were saved.

I lost count of the number of people I buried when they got the fever, and not once did I get it myself. Still today, I thank God for that.

4

February 6, 1624

Last night I tossed and turned in my sleep, plagued with the one fight we had while in the grass plains of Africa. Kayla was at it again, and like a fool I only believed what I wanted to believe. When Cisco wanted to help me carry water for the sick, I screamed at him. For weeks we did not speak. Kayla, of course, used this time to get to him, I thought. Afterwards I knew she had no chance with him. He was devoted only to one woman, me. What a fool I was. And how much precious time we missed.

He was always ready to show me his love in all kinds of ways, to carry me when I was tired, to make sure Rosa-Lee was protected and warm. He was always close by when Faro was in my presence. He never talked directly to me, never even looked at me, but I was always in his thoughts. When he had the opportunity to hunt, he brought back the best meat to me and Rosa- Lee. At night he would cover us with huge leaves just to keep us comfortable and dry.

No matter how exhausted he was I was always his priority. In the weeks we did not speak I would scold myself for mistrusting him. Now I know better. I trust him with everything because I know his love is unchanging. He has not changed since we were married at sea by Captain Derek, the man who rescued us and brought us back to Portugal all those months ago.

What a glorious time that was. After almost two years in the wilds of Africa we were finally rescued by Captain Derek Blanq. He fell in love with Kayla and they got married a month after us. Derek and Cisco became friends on that journey.

†††

On the third day, Rosa-Lee came into Roberto's cabin. The picture of her told him all he wanted to know. Her lips were dry and cracked, and she hungrily eyed the peach he was eating. While stealing glances at the chicken on the table.

"Can I help you, Señorita?" he asked, avoiding her eyes briefly.

"Can I have some water and food, please?" her mouth was so dry that only a whisper was heard over the scratching of the tin plates.

"I cannot hear you, Señorita. Speak up." He lifted his head to meet her eyes.

"Can I have some water and food, please?"

"Will you sit at my table?"

Her expression still showed defiance and anger, but she tried to cover it with exaggerated submissiveness. He smirked.

"Yes."

"Please speak up, I did not hear you."

"Yes, I will sit at your table!"

"Pierre, please bring a chair closer for the Señorita."

Rosa Lee could hardly contain herself. She felt humiliated and infuriated at the same time, but knew she had to give in; just for survival's sake. When a chair was placed behind her, she had to stop herself from grabbing food and water simultaneously. Her lips burned with thirst.

"Do you want water, Señorita?"

"Yes, please." While he poured the sparkling, clean water, she watched his every movement. Every nerve ending in her body shouted cravings for the sweetness. He placed the water carafe back on the table and handed her the cup. With shaking hands, she finished the water in one thirsty gulp. Droplets ran from the side of her mouth. Ochre eyes followed the trail down her neck, over her full bosom and onto her dress.

He had to hand it to her. She had held out for three hot days. The delicate little flower was brave and strong. She reminded him of flowers he once saw blooming in the desert: beautiful and alive with colour, but underneath, hidden under the lush green leaves, thorns waited, and when you tried to pluck one, it would sting you when you least expected it. He had to shift for the stirring that he felt, keeping his expression sternly on her.

She, however, did not notice the stare or the shift. She ate until she was full, the delicious food a welcome treat to her palate. It was quiet for a long time in the captain's cabin with Roberto filling her plate while she ate. Her hands trembling, taking sips of the wine he offered to wash it down. Pierre had already left without her noticing.

Once done, she relaxed, holding the glass of water in her hands, not letting go of the precious fluid, taking frequent sips.

"Meals will be served punctually, every day," he said lazily cleaning his nails with the knife. "I hope, Señorita, that we understand each other better from now on." He met her gaze.

"Without a doubt," she snapped. *Ahh, the thorns,* he smiled.

"Enrico is preparing a bath for you as we speak. Enjoy, Señorita." He smiled at her when she finally let go of the glass.

For the last three days, she received no bath. The heat was unbearable in her cabin, but she refused to go on the upper deck in her state of filth, unkempt hair and alarming body odours.

These men, these savages, will not humiliate me! The only thought that kept her alive.

The bath would be a welcome diversion. She felt sticky from the sea air; her hair hanging listless on her shoulders.

"Thanks, Señor," she said, a bit friendlier. She felt mortified by the experience and she could see that he loved her discomfort. The smirk on his face evident of his thoughts. *"I hate him!"*

"It was a pleasure," he said as she left. She could hear his laugh following her all the way to her door.

"I really hate him."

Two hours later, she felt refreshed and clean, her skin soft and creamy. She decided to go to the upper deck to dry her hair in the midday sun. For the first time since she had come on board, she came up on the deck.

Walking to the bow, a man busy with ropes looked at her with interest. She ignored him, touching the taffrail to keep her balance. She could look far around her, the west coast of Africa noticeable on the horizon. The ship cloves the clear waters. A light sea spray met her that was welcoming in the heat. It was her first time taking a voyage again.

Her mind wandered very far from her immediate surroundings, thinking about a similar voyage twenty years ago when she was only four years old. Memories flooded back; of how they had met the giant they now knew as Cisco Almaida. She remembered how she ran up to him, telling him that she would be his daughter because he didn't have one and looked sad. From that day forward there was a bond between that sailor, now her father, and herself.

She remembered hugging his thick leg, feeling safe. His hug in return was hesitant because the captain did not allow any contact between the passengers and the crew. In her young mind she was unaware of the trouble she had caused him, only that she had a longing for a father figure. Her father was never interested in her, never around, or when he was, he was always drunk. She had always been afraid of her biological father and had never had the liberty to run up to him and hug him as she could with the giant.

Her young heart immediately reached out to him. He talked to her in a soft, low voice, and even today, he never raised his voice to her, even when she knew she deserved it. He was a loving, gentle giant, and she loved him fiercely.

In her eyes, he was everything a father, a husband, and a man should be. She remembered how he was whipped because he held her, the pain on his rugged face, but not once did he cry out. His back ripped open from the lashes but still he smiled at her.

Her mother thought that she didn't witness it, but she did and when it was finished, she sat in a corner and she cried about the unfairness of the grownups. Her biological father stood close by and laughed when the giant received the beating and she hated him. Never once did she seek for his affection or love again throughout the voyage.

In the year and a half that they were in the bush country of Africa and she got scared, she always ran to the giant seeking safety and comfort in his arms.

Cisco was always there.

Ever since her mother and he met, they had loved each other dearly. It did not matter how hard they tried to ignore it. Their feelings became stronger over the long period. They never could openly express their love because of the "no contact" rule that the captain enforced harshly on them. No one ever loved that man, not even her father, who was always in a drunken stupor because of all the idle time at sea. He had nothing to keep him busy except gambling with the sailors.

This was the first time, after their ordeal that she was back on the open sea. For the last twenty years she went on board ships only because her father wanted to teach her the science of chart reading and making knots, but she had never gone on a voyage again.

She was happy on their estate, helping in the villa and in the village. She loved nature and the smell of freshly worked ground as well as the peace and tranquillity that it brought to her soul.

Sadly, she wondered if she would ever set eyes on that place again. Things at sea could change very quickly. She knew the sea was never a friend.

She remembered when Manuel and Pedro were born and how happy Mama and Papa were. Before they were born, her father had always had a longing in his piercing eyes. But after their birth it disappeared, replaced by contentment and joy. He always told them how much he loved them, and her mother had developed into a beautiful woman because of the love he had shown her. Before their marriage her mother had been called an "ice queen." She lived a bitter and lonely life. That changed after she married the gentle giant.

One day Rosa-Lee would also have a love like that. At the age of twenty-four, she was still not married, but her hopes for the right man to come had not wavered. Many suitors came and spoke to her father about her hand in marriage, but he always respected her wishes. He never gave in to the demanding men and she loved him even more.

To be loved like that was her one goal. She wanted to be protected and to feel safe in the arms of the man she loved, to trust him. That was the love she sought.

Now she found herself on a ship on her way to the harem of a pirate captain on an island very far from her beloved family. There was no way that her life would end this way. She could not accept this.

Tears of frustration ran down her cheeks. She never thought that this would ever happen to her; that she would be part of a price to set her brother free.

Finally, when the evening bell announced the dinner, she was once again aware of her surroundings. She wiped her face clean from the dry tears and went down to the dining cabin. She did not keep track of the time she spent on deck nor realize that it had gotten so late.

With a gentle stroke to her still loose, wavy hair, shoulders straight and back rigid, she walked into the dining cabin. The men were already seated, but the moment they noticed her they stood up, waiting for her to take a seat in the middle of the table. She acknowledged their gesture with a simple nod of the head and sat down.

The captain sat at the head of the table. Pierre, the chief mate, Alexi, Enrico and two other men sat around her. The captain nodded in her direction and they started the meal. The men were in deep conversation. She listened with half an ear, keeping her eyes on her plate, eating the deliciously prepared food consisting of roast beef and vegetables. When she was almost done with the meal, the captain addressed her.

"Do you feel better after the bath and the stroll on the deck, Señorita?" Looking forlorn and far away Roberto wondered about the sadness. He wished he could reach out to her, but he knew that it would be futile at that moment.
Remember the thorns.

"Yes, thank you." Her eyes were still downcast on the plate before her as she took small bites of the remaining food. The men continued with the conversation and she listened, still half-heartedly.

Roberto watched her from across the table. Not once did she make eye contact with anyone present. He wondered what she was thinking about. From her brother's stories, he knew that this was her first voyage after their ordeal. *Could it still be difficult for her?*

He had watched her the entire afternoon as she stood on the deck, her thoughts far from the present. Emotions played on her face that brought her to tears. He wanted to go closer and comfort her, but he knew he would not have been welcomed. She never once noticed him, so close to her, and he could enjoy her beauty without any disturbances.

She reminded him of his mother. His mother was also beautiful as a young woman and caring. She had strength in her that no one could break, and through many difficult times she was the one who kept them focused. He missed his parents; it was now sixteen years since he had last seen them. Ever since he had met the young señorita he found himself longing for a family; a family he could call his own.

Yes, this woman intrigued him on a completely different level. He knew many women in the different harbours all over the known world; beautiful women who captured his interest for a while. He would have his time with them, but when he left, he never thought about them again.

This one, Rosa-Lee Almaida, captivated him even before he met her, but to know her as a warm, passionate woman would be wonderful and fulfilling.

He could see himself on a farm with her by his side, building a future with her. He even imagined a few children running around, enjoying the fruit of his labour.

For so long he had suppressed thoughts like that, but he thought about it more and more often, enjoying the comfort it brought to him. Since he had seen her, he knew she would be the one. She could be wild and passionate. She would keep him on his toes, but he would keep her in his arms. He would take her and make her his. She would come alive, begging him to satisfy her every need. She would be a wild cat, and he could not wait to tame her.

The life he led had been forced upon him at a very young age. It was the only way that he could help his parents and save the farm. And for this lady sitting across from him, he was willing to give it up. From the life of a pirate he longed to go back to be a farmer. From the very first moment he saw her, he knew they were meant to meet. He would have her and somehow, he would have to convince her and the Falcon of this.

He knew what the Falcon had planned for her. Her father was correct in expecting the worse. Her fate would lead to death if he did not intervene. The Falcon's way with women was legendary, using them, breaking them until there was nothing left of the once beautiful woman. Not a very pretty picture.

The Falcon was a brute when it came to women. He only enjoyed them for a while and then threw them to his men. Roberto had seen women broken emotionally and physically by the Falcon and to see this woman in his hands? He would not allow it. He would rather carry her away to a remote island and marry her, than for her to experience that kind of abuse.

†††

February 28, 1624

Today I had to deal with a situation in the village as part of land owner duties. It left me sick to my stomach and brought back memories best forgotten.

We stumbled on another African village, not deserted this time. At first the people were friendly, allowing our surviving group of twenty-five to camp and eat with them. For two days we could rest and have shelter. Qonchita started to get her colour back and Kayla began to explore. But that cost her dearly. One of the village men had his eyes on her since the day we got there. And when opportunity knocked, he took it.

He cornered her near the kraal and assaulted her. The next morning when I found her, I was angry. I went straight to the chief's hut to demand justice. And in return he demanded Kayla as his wife. I could not allow this. Kayla was still very young, and I felt responsible for her. Although a seductive temptress, she did not deserve to be treated in that manner and be left behind.

When Captain Breno died of the fever and the people elected me as their leader I vowed that no one would be left behind again. I begged for her release and finally one of the slave girls offered to stay behind. It was touch and go for a moment and I really thought that was where we all would die. For a long time, Kayla was not the same but with gentle coaching from Qonchita she made it through.

Once again Qonchita came through for this young woman and I really hope she will pull through. Tomorrow I must speak to the parents of the young man and hope we can come to a fair arrangement.

5

March 16, 1624

The past month Cisco was met with many challenges from the villagers. He was confronted by other land owners who did not feel the same as he did in managing the land. He is exhausted by the continuous strain, but I have faith in him and know he will do the best for us and our people.

He learns fast and with Franco guiding him I know he can only succeed. He is now an accomplish rider and he and Furor are seen all over the estate, dashing over the plains at breakneck speed. Furor's enthusiasm is contagious. The other horses, especially Rosa-Lee's pony, are a struggle to contain in the stable.

The baby is growing fast, and I struggle to walk properly. This is much to Cisco's delight, but he demands that I rest as often as possible. He even gave the staff instructions to keep a close eye on me when he is not here. I miss him when he leaves in the mornings to do his work but the reunion at night makes up for it.

His tenderness towards me on one occasion reminds me when we were in the heart of Africa. We travelled for weeks by foot after we left yet another village. Many of our people, including the captain, had died of the fever and Cisco was the official leader. By his estimate we were very close to a fort in Mozambique and he decided to take several men and walk to the Fort to get some help. Our food levels were low, and he made sure that there was enough to eat and drink before he left with eight other men.

He left Alfonso in charge and the small group of twenty-four people were grateful for the rest. But the moment they left the fever once again swept through the group. Soon everyone was in a terrible state, with only me, Kayla and Alfonso to tend to the sick. We buried people and by the fourth week only six remained. Faro himself was on his last breath and during this time we made peace. Rosa-Lee visited him often. The once brusque and impatient man turned into a loving father. I had a hard time with this. My loyalty and love belonged to Cisco, but I was still married to Faro. During one night of clarity he told me he welcomed the fact that I found love. He asked for forgiveness for the hard and cruel times I had endured under him. In a sense we made peace, but I could never love him. My heart was in turmoil because I knew I could not leave Cisco and never see him again. That was my train of thought all awhile Cisco was gone.

I missed him. Rosa-Lee missed him. I did the best I could and placed my feelings and concerns in the back of my mind while tending to the sick. Starved and tired, we went on. By then when someone passed away, I simply covered the body, since every man was either dead or too sick to bury them.

Alfonso got sick and I was busy attending to him when Cisco and a small group of men appeared out of the bushes. It was not the same group that left with him. My heart went on a rampage the moment I saw him. He stood there, dumbfounded at the sight he saw. He searched for me and did not recognise me. At that stage I was a walking skeleton. My beauty had faded, my skin was like sandpaper and darker than normal. My once soft black hair was all tangled and without life.

He was rested, and very handsome in a new pair of clothing. The signs of our ordeal were still visible on him. But the moment he saw me, he wrapped me in his arms. I cried, not caring about the people and what they might say. For the second time since I knew him, he kissed me. I would never forget that kiss. If there was any doubt in my mind left, he demolished it completely with that kiss.

Later when we calmed down and settled with the food he had brought, Faro called us over.

He said that he would no longer stand in our way and gave his blessing. From that day forward Cisco and Faro became friends until Faro's death at sea weeks later.

We did have a disagreement a few days later our way to the fort. I was so weak I could not walk, my feet troubling me once again. I expected his help, but he was too busy to attend to me and ignored me, I was furious. But a week later Cisco convinced me of his love again. In my frail and weak state, I easily saw things differently than what they were. Now we can laugh about it but then it was serious. It took a spider to bring me to my senses.

†††

When Rosa-Lee finally stood up to leave the cabin Roberto followed her and asked, "Would you care to go up and walk with me on the deck?"

Hazelnut eyes met ochre ones and for a few seconds they just locked before she answered, her eyes revealing her shock at the invitation.

"Yes, I would like that." It was still early, and she was not in the mood to confine herself in her cabin. After three days of self-imposed lock-up, she wanted to feel the wind in her hair and the sea spray on her face. The fact that he asked her to walk with him shocked her the most.

Be alert Rosa-Lee. He cannot be trusted!

Darkness filled the starry night sky. The quarter moon made it even darker. Lit lanterns on the upper deck added a romantic feeling, she thought, not a scene she was comfortable sharing with the pirate.

You could barely see anything out on the sea as they walked along the taffrail on the deck. Only the sound of the ship breaking through the waters interrupted the silence. The few men that were on duty were quiet, nodding when they passed. If she did not know better, she would have thought that they were alone.

"Your brother has told me a lot of stories about what you endured during your adventures into Africa. Don't you want to tell me a story?"

She glanced at him but could not see his face clearly, covered in darkness, his hands clasped behind his back. He sounded sincere in his request and his presence calmed her, especially his mentioning her brother. She asked hesitantly, "You know my brother?"

"Yes. I have spoken with him a few times."

"Was he still fine when you left?"

"Yes, he was," came the honest reply. "Please, tell me a story," he repeated, looking at her.

Rosa-Lee felt liberated. The fear of her brother's well-being kept her motivated during the 3 days locked in the cabin. Now the tension left her body. Strangely she believed the stranger and looked at him sideways for a moment. His gaze still fixated on her.

To avoid him she stared out over the dark sea; deep in thought. Emotions playing over the youthful face.

Just when Roberto thought she wasn't going to tell him something she began to relate a story very familiar to her.

"A horrific storm came up near the north-eastern coast of Africa. The waves were higher than the ship and they towered over us terrifyingly, with a fierce and menacing anger. Promising to crush us with every pounding." He could see she was reliving it, as she closed her eyes.

"The wind was cold. It felt like it wanted to tear the skin from our faces. I was never as terrified as I was that night, clutching to my mother's body. People cried out that we were going to die. But my mother covered my ears to silence the voices around us.

"Someone yelled that they must drink the liquor so that at least they would be drunk enough to dull the moment they drowned. People were stampeding all over the ship as if they were possessed, clambering to the barrels on the lower deck. Everyone was forced to drink; even the slaves that were shackled to the ship's hull. With their heads forced into the liquid, many drowned under the pressure when they tried to resist. Blood mixed with the liquor, but people still drank it. I will never forget the madness of that night. The fear that gripped us was so real that I cried tears mingled with the salty water."

"Finally, when land was visible, my father shouted that a rowboat had to go to the shore with a rope. A few still able to think with clarity reacted immediately. Once the rope was secured, those ashore sent a signal. Father strapped me to his back and my mother to his chest and jump into the angry, cold waves."

"I held on to him with everything that I had. My mother never made a sound from in front of him. A few times, we went under into the cold depths, and just barely in time, emerged again. Father saved us that day without wavering. Back then he was only a sailor who owed us nothing, but he took care of us. He was unselfish, and we felt safe with him."

"From the first moment I saw him, I accepted him as my father and to him I was the daughter he never had. He was always gentle and kind to me. He and my mother are inseparable, even to this day."

A soft sob left her mouth and she stopped talking. The emotions very intense in her.

Roberto waited next to her. His hands clasped behind his back, he could hear her struggling for control. His own control broke and without thinking, he placed an arm around the soft, delicate shoulders.

She stiffened and stood still under his touch, his arm warm and soft on her bare skin, giving her a feeling of safety.

She looked at him now standing closer to her and she could see tenderness and understanding in his face. This was a contrast to everything she knew about this man. The stern and menacing look from the last three days had vanished. For a moment, she enjoyed the closeness they shared before she stepped away and he dropped his arm.

"He sounds like a great man and I would love to actually meet him one day," he said softly, the sternness gone from his voice. He had a beautiful, calming voice: strong and steady.

"He is a great man and father, and a wonderful husband to my mother. I miss him awfully. I miss both my parents."

"Maybe one day you will meet a man like that as well, Si?"

"You confuse me, Captain."

"My name is Roberto, not Captain," he said with a chuckle.

"You confuse me Roberto," she said, but with a grim smile.

"I have heard that many times, Señorita." He removed a strand of hair from her face, at the same moment she moved to put it behind her ear. Their hands met, and he folded hers into his warm grasp, bringing it to his lips.

"Good night Rosa-Lee. Thanks for the story."

Stunned by the intimate gesture, shivers went up her spine, shivers she never felt before. Amazed, she could only watch him.

I must hate him! He is a pirate! She reminded herself. She removed her hand and abruptly said, "Good night Roberto."

I will have to find a way to get free and help my brother. She thought as she watched his retreating back. To stay here would be devasting for her.

†††

April 18, 1624

Today I held my son in my arms for the first time. Manuel Francisco Almaida. I am a father now. My heart is too big for my chest. I, Cisco Almaida, once an ordinary sailor, am now the father of a beautiful daughter and a son. How fortunate I am to have my family. My dreams have changed into reality and I can love and enjoy them every day.

Qonchita was in labour for ten hours, ten agonizing hours, but it was worth it. She is even more beautiful than before. Once again, she has blessed me beyond measure. How fortunate and happy I am.

Rosa-Lee is ecstatic about her new brother. She wants to help with everything. What a sweet, strong-willed child. She is everything I wanted in a daughter and more. I can hardly wait to teach them all I know, about the sea, the land, about people.

My family.

6

May 6, 1624

Manuel had a bit of a fever today and we were really frightened, but the medicine woman assured us not to worry and gave us some powder to feed him. He is a strong boy, already opening his eyes and watching the world go by.

Cisco is a joy to watch as he carries the infant from room to room. Rosa-Lee is always close by to see when she can have the opportunity to hold her brother. I normally must fight for time between the two. But it does not bother me at the least. To see Cisco this happy is more than worth it.

I remember other babies we buried in the heart of Africa, along with their parents, due to fever, babies that never had the chance to grow and experience life. This is what makes Manuel so special, to experience life through him in a greater measure.

We remember those frightful days as if it was yesterday. The heat, the insect-infested time, coupled with the fever and constant rains. I felt it would never stop. Through it all we had to hope that help would come or that we would find a haven. But it took us some time to come to that place.

Help never came and we were on our own. We wandered through that wilderness in a daze. I can barely remember the sights around me. All I remember was the continued effort to survive in an unkind and untamed wilderness.

No more. I would never return to that place.

†††

"Sails ahoy!" the call from the crow master resounded from the main mast four days later. Sails appeared on the horizon, coming closer with each passing hour.

Rosa-Lee was excited about the prospect of seeing another ship. Maybe she could send a word or get some help. When she ran onto the deck, the ship, named the *Heerengardt* was closer, and she saw the ensign of the D.E.I.C. fluttering in the soft wind. The *Heerengardt* was much larger in build carrying two hundred soldiers and crew, canons, merchandise and coins than the *Contra O Vento*, a frigate built for speed and manoeuvrability with only eighty crew members.

Roberto and his men's faces were tense as they scurried around to change the flags from pirate to her father's crest ensign.

"They want permission to come on board," the crow master yelled down.

"They can come," Roberto yelled back, and he signalled back with the burgee.

The *Contra O Vento* was prepared to accept the visit, making sure all signs of piracy were gone. All the men knew what was expected from them; to act like regular sailors on a ship of this size. When the long boat came closer, an idea filled Rosa-Lee and she descended to her cabin below, unnoticed.

A while later, the captain of the D.E.I.C vessel, a man of impressive frame, stepped on deck. His fierce look pierced through everyone and everything. However, Roberto was not intimidated by the man and met his fierce gaze only with a slight degree of humbleness. Both men assessing each other as both bowed in chivalry.

A young sailor moved closer to the captain and his men. With his hat pulled low over his face, he moved forward unnoticed until he mingled with the strangers. It seemed that he was a part of the crew, staring at his shoes. He made no sound and no eye contact.

"Captain Peek du Toit at your service." The deep voice of the captain filled the air. He looked around him with piercing grey eyes, missing nothing.

"Where are you going?" he demanded

"Captain Roberto of the *Contra O Vento*. We are going to India to meet one of our ships and escort it back to Portugal," Roberto replied in a confident voice.

"Can I see the papers?"

"Yes." Roberto handed him their manifesto. The tall man took the papers and inspected them, fingering the names listed.

"All seems in order. May I walk around?"

"Yes, please do. We always welcome the D.E.I.C visits."

"How is Almaida?"

"At home and well."

"What is wrong with the ship you plan to escort?"

"It ran into trouble after a storm. We are on our way to help."

Roberto only answered the necessary questions and did not offer any further details. From a distance, his crew watched everything in silence. They were alert, their gaze fixed on the ship in front of them.

When the inspection was completed, the men exchanged a few words and then walked back to where Roberto was standing.

"Is everything in order?" Roberto asked.

"Everything seems fine. We have received numerous reports of piracy in these waters. We must be careful and inspect each vessel."

"I understand. We will be on the lookout for any pirates. Thanks for the warning, Señor." And he made a slight bow.

"Good. We will be off so that you can continue with your voyage."

"Thank you, Señor, and goodbye." They watched the men very carefully as they descended the Jacob's ladder, entered their long boat, and rowed back to their ship. His men were highly alert, looking for any trouble.

However, he could swear that there were six men on the rowboat before, and now there were seven. *"How did I miss one?"* Everything seemed in order. All his men were accounted for. Slowly he relaxed, and Pierre gave the signal that they could continue.

As he walked to his grand cabin Roberto was deep in thought. Something wasn't right. He could feel it, but he could not put his finger on it yet. Sitting at his mahogany desk, he pored over the charts, making sure they were still on course. With the manifest open before him, he wrote down the time and date of Captain Peek du Toit's visit.

At suppertime Rosa-Lee's absences was evident. Her empty chair stared at him. Furious, he sent word to Enrico.

"Where is Señorita Almaida?"

"Not in her cabin, Captain," Enrico replied cautiously. "I have looked everywhere but I cannot find her." He tried to appease Roberto. Enrico was clearly distracted and fearful fidgeting with his pants, his eyes down cast. The man in front of him was not easily fooled. Enrico had warned the señorita, after he had found her in her cabin dressed in men's clothing, of the foolishness of she was about to do. But she would not listen to him and he could not lie to this man.

"Did you look on every deck?"

"Yes, Captain." Sweat formed on the boy's forehead and upper lip as the captain looked at him through narrowed eyes.

"What are you not telling me, Enrico?" Roberto barked; all his usual brusque sternness back. Then it dawned on Roberto who the seventh person was. He cursed as he turned to Pierre with a quick move causing the chair to be unbalanced for a moment.

"She is on the other ship!" He slammed his fist down on the table. The plates and glasses rattled, and a bottle of wine toppled over. Pierre caught it just in time.

"We will have to go and get her. For this she will pay," he said, seething and pacing the floor. "She was disguised as one of the men. She has put us all in danger with her game. We will have to get her back." he explained to his men.

"That will be a daring feat," Pierre said.

"I realize that, but we have no choice. If she talks, we are all dead."

"Who says she didn't talk already?" Pierre asked carefully.

"Then the ship would have returned. We are not that far from the *Heerengardt* that it cannot catch up with us. We will have to follow and devise a plan to reclaim her without them noticing it. It is a good thing that the moon is not shining tonight."

"Roberto! You are mad to suggest this. We will be going into the heart of a D.E.I.C ship and if they catch us, we would be immediately hanged."

"I will go alone," Roberto said thoughtfully. This undertaking was of the highest risk.

With the order given they turned, following the ship with speed and in absolute dark silence. All the pirates were on the lookout for any movement, eyes darting over the black calm waters, searching for the *Heerengardt*.

It took them six hours to intercept the *Heerengardt*. By then the sun was already dawning in rich amber colours and Roberto realized they could not get closer without being noticed. They fell back, keeping their distance with the crow master giving feedback every hour.

†††

June 11, 1624

Kayla came for a short visit. She really looked well considering she was five months pregnant. Derek was overwhelmed, keeping a tight hold on her hands.

She in turn could not get enough of little Manuel. Not that I could blame her. He was growing strong and healthy. Every day he looked more and more like me with the exception that he had his mother's dark brooding eyes. He was big for his two months, but it was normal, the medicine woman assured me.

Today we relived many of the moments we shared with them in the wilderness of Africa. Kayla remembered the time that one of the chiefs hunted us and we had to hide. He wanted Qonchita as his woman and I was not willing to let her go; under no circumstances. We had to flee late at night. The rest of the group scattered in a different direction.

Then when we finally came back to the group, I was accused of abandoning the group and punished accordingly. Both Qonchita and Kayla were angry at the captain. But I took my punishment and made the best of it. Qonchita forgot all about propriety and rebuked me because I was so calm about it. I explained to her that the Captain had rules, and it did look as if I was running away.

For days she did not speak to me and today I can admit that it brought my heart much happiness. I knew she loved me, but she never showed it openly. That only revealed her real feelings. Faro of course was angry with her for openly choosing me over him and he shunned her for a few days.

Then came the event that changed everything between Qonchita and Kayla. Two weeks later we were again facing a stubborn chief who helped as at first but in the end demanded to have the women for himself. I never had to think so quickly as on that day. I stripped Qonchita and Kayla before him and showed their state. Since all four of his women were overweight, I pointed out how skinny Qonchita and Kayla were. This displeased him greatly.

Two slave woman that still had enough fat on them said they would stay, and this pleased the chief. In Africa you learn to think on your feet and use the tools you have. All finesse and veneer are stripped away and all that is left is survival. You don't think, you just act and hope it was the best thing. Sometimes all you have left is your instincts to act on.

That means live or die. For Qonchita and Rosa-Lee I would do anything if it meant they were safe.

7

August 22, 1624

Today was exceptionally warm day. The humid air caused our clothes to cling to our sweat-drenched bodies. Manuel was uncomfortable with the heat until Cisco took him to the river and dipped him feet first in. For the first time in days he was happy, laughing as his father dragged him through the water playfully. Rosa-Lee also joined them in the water and I sat safely at the side with my feet in the stream.

It was a glorious summer day and Cisco relaxed with the children. He was extremely busy this time of the year. The responsibilities of a land owner weighed heavily on him. There was trouble with other land owners, and they had held meetings the week before. It irritated him greatly since it took him away from his home and family. Also, there were problems with the villagers he had to sort out. Tomorrow he must leave for Lisbon to see to the loading of the shipment he is sending to India.

Alfonso arrived a week ago and is helping him. The two friends were happy to see each other again for the first time since we arrived eight months ago.

Alfonso is captain of the new ship Cisco received from the D.E.I.C. in tribute for his bravery during the two years we struggled through the wilderness. If it was not for him, we would not have made it and would have perished with the rest of the crew and slaves. Alfonso had no qualms about resigning from his old ship. He took the job Cisco offered since he receives part of the profits as payment.

Alfonso met a young woman in India that he brought with him. It was easy to see the sailor was smitten with her. He is talking about marriage before he leaves in another two weeks.

Akanksha is a raven-haired beauty with big, wide, smouldering eyes in such a youthful face. She loves Alfonso as much as he does her, which we are thankful for.

Previously another woman just wanted his name for her unborn child. He thought it was his until the baby was born. Cisco said that Alfonso was shocked and turned his attentions away from any woman. It was really a pity since he is a fine man.

Now he has met Akanksha after all these years and it seems he finally has his own joy. I wish them all the happiness in the world. Since he would be at sea often, she will stay in India, where he has already purchased a house for her. She is very shy, but I did manage to speak to her and help her buy her trousseau with the aid of Alfonso, since she could only speak Portuguese with great difficulty.

We all deserved happiness in our lives, finally putting the last two years out of our minds. Nightmares still woke me during the night. The sounds and smells of people dying were embedded in our minds.

Thankfully Rosa-Lee adjusted well and her nightmares become fewer and fewer.

†††

It was a clear day with brilliant sunlight. They could see the *Heerengardt* through the binoculars as they kept pace with the larger vessel through the vast deep blue Atlantic. The ocean was calm as small waves broke against the bow and a light breeze in the sails pushing them forward, closer to the *Heerengardt*.

Roberto was seething as he looked in the direction of the horizon where he knew the ship with Rosa-Lee was. With not much to do but hope that she would not betray them. *How could she do this?* He thought the last four days had changed things. Fool that he was, he had trusted her. What could she do on the ship, surrounded by ocean?

He never thought she could do this.

"Never underestimate your enemy or a woman," Falcon always said. "Sly foxes," he called them.

Thorns. Roberto gritted his teeth. *Thorns.*

Pierre tried to talk to him, but Roberto was not in a conversational mood. Pierre let him be. They went through the tasks of running the ship in silence.

It seemed that they were headed for the islands of Cape Verde, islands Roberto knew very well. He had raided them a few times himself. His bet was that they would anchor at the island of Santiago, a place he would investigate. But why would a ship from the D.E.I.C stop there? It did not make sense. Normally they just left the islanders to themselves. Again, a nagging feeling settled in his gut. But for now, all he could do was wait patiently for night-time, when they would be able to get closer.

By the time lunch was served, clouds had begun to accumulate in the clear sky. The shoreline would not be the safest place to be with such unpromising-looking clouds. Nevertheless, the

Heerengardt continued its course and they were forced to follow.

With dangerously low clouds hanging over the waters, by sunset Roberto knew they had trouble. But he could not take the risk of being discovered, and he had to get Rosa-Lee back. *She will pay for this foolishness he thought once again.*

"Roberto, don't you think we must turn away?" Pierre asked during supper. "We are entering dangerous waters. The señorita has had enough time to tell them about us. We need to get away while there is still time."

Roberto ate his meal, tasting nothing of the delicious food. He listened to every argument his lieutenant had, and they made sense. But he could not leave her, even if she did deceive them. He knew their lives were in danger. The D.E.I.C was an organization that had no tolerance for pirates; and then there was the brewing storm.

Would she be safe?

The past four days, while she told him more stories, he knew the sea disaster twenty years ago still lingered in the back of her mind. It did not matter how brave or strong she was, the upcoming storm would devastate her. He knew that much. He had begun to care about her, to be protective of her, fearful for her safety.

Would she be all right among the sailors? He asked himself once again, would they treat her like the lady she is?

If they touched her...he clenched his fists. He did not want to think about it. He knew what he would do but also knew the consequences of such a brutal act. The pain and loss were unbearable at times. He wanted her back on the *Contra O Vento*, back with him. His possessiveness a new feeling he struggled with the last few days. Now, he missed her presence.

These were the thoughts that he struggled with. He was also in a place where he made decisions for them all. His men were his responsibility.

"I hear you Pierre, but we need to get her back. My father will kill me if I lose her."

"He will understand."

"No, Pierre, you know he will not. It's his laws, remember?"

Pierre sighed, shaking his head. "Are we still getting her from the ship?"

"Yes."

"And the storm?"

"We better hope it will give us enough time to bring her back safely before it hits."

"I will ready the longboat. Who will go with us?"

"Just us. I don't want anyone else in danger." Pierre nodded. No point in arguing. Physically both he and Roberto can do it. Because of the storm, it would help to have some extra muscle, but he was the captain. Yes, he knew Falcon. He was as bad as they came.

It was after eight, the sky so dark you could hardly see your hand in front of your face. Silently they approached the *Heerengardt*. Her lanterns gave them enough light to follow and get as close as possible.

They had only this window of opportunity and they had to take it or lose Rosa-Lee forever. Her life and theirs were at stake. Although Roberto was the son of the Falcon, the Falcon would not hesitate to kill him for disobeying a direct order.

With the long boat prepared, ready and on the water, Roberto and Pierre were over the railing in no time. The waves were higher around the boat and rocked it slightly, but they were used to it. They began rowing, with one eye on the *Heerengardt* four miles ahead of them and one eye on the dark foreboding clouds above them which turned the heavens pitch-black. They rowed with gentle strokes, making sure that the oars did not splash in the water as they slowly drew closer

The wind picked up, working with them, but they knew the return part would be harder, and hoped that they would find her in time. He and Pierre had talked about that in detail. They were both familiar with D.E.I.C ships. Their large scale might make it almost impossible. It would not be easy to locate her, for she could be in numerous places.

They would have to take their chances and should play everything by ear; but by the looks of it the *Heerengardt* was quiet.

Finally, after another hour of rowing, they reached the ship. Making sure that the longboat was tied securely by the ropes hanging down, they left their boots in the boat. With strong arms, they pulled themselves up onto the rope they had secured, daggers in their mouths ready for any danger. When Roberto crawled over the railing onto the deck, all was quiet. Two lanterns hung near the boatswain sleeping at the wheel. His soft snores a sure sign of deep sleep.

Eyes darting around on the lighted deck, they saw one other man sitting in the shadows, smoking his cheroot. Grey puffs released into the dark night air, away from the cabins.

They moved forward on the balls of their feet, making no sound on the sleeping ship. Their muscles were tired of the exercise, but they forced themselves to move forward. A trained eye could only see the crow master and he was looking far-off in the distance, hopefully not in the direction of the *Contra O Vento*. They would have to move swiftly and not draw any attention toward themselves.

"You will wait here, and I will go. I have a good idea where she will be," Roberto whispered to Pierre. Although it would be quicker if they both searched on a ship this size, it was better to keep a trained eye on the men on the upper deck. Pierre could warn him of any lurking dangers. Again, Roberto had to speculate about the ship and its crew. The normal military alertness and precision were not evident. There were no guards, and it made him wary.

Using the dark night as cover Roberto sneaked through the shadows to the stairs leading to the lower deck where the crew was sleeping. Except for the ship moving through the relatively calm waters, no other sound filtered through. Men were hanging in their hammocks, snoring.

Once again, not an expected manner of the D.E.I.C and he frowned, squatting on the balls of his feet, to make sure that everything was as it should be. He made sure that his eyes were accustomed to the dark before he moved further.

Silently he moved again and managed to pass all the sleeping men and down the next stairs taking him deeper into the hull into the farthest point in the lower deck. He searched behind every crate and sack until he recognized her small posture behind a large heavy crate. To a normal eye, she could go for a young boy, but his trained eye recognized her. The small manicured hands were a dead giveaway. She lay in the shadows with her back to the wooden wall and stacks of bags around her.

She had tried to cover herself, but her long hair had slipped from the hat's brim and her shirt revealed more than she would've liked. For a moment he just took in the sight. Hovering over her, he could see she was in a deep sleep and he wondered why she had not revealed herself to the men. She could then have slept in one of the cabins in the castle, not here trying to hide away.

He hoped they hadn't done anything to her because, if they had, he would kill them. Precaution be damned. He grimaced at the thought.

Something had to have spooked her to make her keep herself hidden. He wondered what it could have been.

When he reached her, he covered her mouth so that she could not make a sound when she awoke. Startled at the hold on her mouth she awoke and recognized him. She moved slightly and released a soft moan but with one swift expert strike, he knocked her unconscious and then flung her over his shoulders. He looked around to make sure the sound did not attract any unwanted guests. Satisfied and without a word, he carried her out. Not one sailor had moved.

She was like a feather on his shoulder, so he could easily manoeuvre up the stairs and through the sleeping men without making a sound. Staying on his toes, he quickly walked to the stairs and onto the upper deck where Pierre waited. Giving him a thumbs up, he let Pierre know everything was good.

Once more, he furrowed his brows. The entire scene didn't make sense but left it. He could not express his concerns to Pierre because the conversation would attract attention. Yet it was puzzling.

Another three hours passed as they rowed against the wind. Pierre always kept his eyes on the Heerengardt until they reached the *Contra O Vento*. It was a painfully slow journey.

"Did you also find it very strange?" Roberto whispered when they were a safe distance away.

"Yes," came the reply.

"An unguarded D.E.I.C ship in the middle of the ocean? It does not add up."

"Yes, I looked around while you were on the lower deck. No guards present in a ship of that size. It is alarming."

"What could it mean?"

"Not sure, but the señorita here had to know because she was hiding when I found her." Roberto gave the small bundel a sideways glance, deep in thought.

"Really?" and Pierre raised a brow.

"Yes." They row in silence for a while before Pierre said: "Well, this will be interesting to hear."

"Yes." Roberto watched the unconscious face, a very beautiful unconscious face sternly. For a moment he allowed himself to grin at her bravery before the stern, blank look was back, not revealing anything of his inner turmoil.

†††

December 24, 1624

It has been a year since our ordeal, and here in Portugal on the estate time has passed quickly. Our second Christmas together as a family is already here. So many blessings to be grateful for.

The children are growing, especially Rosa-Lee who will one day be a beautiful young woman, a very feisty, strong willed woman, perfect in every way.

I pray that the right man will be worthy of her, that she will find the joy in marriage as I have found. Marriage is everything if you can share it with the one you love. I will take great care to give her the opportunity to meet such a man.

It will be a special man who will be able to love her and respect her for who she is.

My brave little Rosa-Lee, who brightens my days.

8

April 01, 1625

We are expecting our second child. The medicine woman confirmed my suspicions today. Cisco is overwhelmed once again.

In a few days Manuel will be one year old. What a beautiful, handsome boy. He walks everywhere. He loves being outside and amongst the animals.

Everyone says he will be a farmer one day. Cisco is teaching him everything he knows. Sometimes I must remind him the child was only one this year. But he is convinced Manuel understands him and continues with the lessons. How could I refuse him the pleasure of being a father? Cisco fills my days with happiness.

What more could I ask?

†††

The *Contra O Vento* sailed away in the opposite direction from the *Heerengardt*. The threatening clouds had finally released their waters the moment they had stepped back on deck. The still-unconscious señorita hung over the broad shoulders of the pirate captain. Men watched the procession as they walked down the main stairs to the lower deck.

Roberto's face was grim as he laid her down on her bed in the cabin.

He dismissed Pierre and sat for the rest of the night in the chair in front of the small mahogany desk, watching her sleeping figure. She looked small and fragile on the bed. Tired lines marked the filthy young face. Creases marred her forehead and dark circles under her eyes paled her normal rosy cheeks. One hand rested under her cheek as she slept. He could not help but to admire her again.

When he had patted her down, he had found her pistol and knife and locked it in his trunk for safekeeping. There were no visible signs of struggles on her, other than the fact that she was tired, and he bet, hungry as well.

Why did she hide? The captain of the vessel would have helped her unless something spooked her.

His mind was racing, realizing in how much danger she had been, and his anger rose once again, for her foolishness and the danger she had put them all in. Too angry to sleep, although his muscles ached after the strenuous exercise, he stared at her form in men's clothing. Her shapely legs drew his attention. The curve of her breasts was visible in perfect roundness under the shirt. Three open buttons revealed her delicate skin. His body demanded attention. He paced the floor in discomfort and drank wine.

The room smelled like her, lavender and something sweet, a smell he did not know but had already grown accustomed to it. His imagination was running wild with things he wanted to do to her.

When daylight coloured the water, he saw her stir in her sleep. He waited patiently for her to wake, the fear and anger still raging within.

This would be interesting.

†††

When Rosa-Lee awoke, she was in her cabin and the sun was just making its presence known. Tied to the bed pulling at the restrains, she tried to move, but could not.

"You finally decided to join us?"

A stern, angry voice spoke directly in front of her. She lifted her head and looked straight at him, still in a daze. Her head wanted to split in two. The agony of the last two days, without food or water followed by the blow against her head felt like torture. His menacing eyes piercing through her made her fearful of the man dressed in black. His appearance was perfect. Dark hair tucked behind an ear and the meanest look she had ever seen on him. She trembled with fear yet was happy she was back.

She could only stare at him as she wet her drying lips, reliving the past twenty-four hours.

She had quickly realized that she had made a mistake once she stepped on board of the *Heerengardt*. The captain was not who he said he was and there was a look of utter disgust on his face, which made his face repulsive.

When he spoke to his crew, she immediately thought of the cruel Captain Breno who was cruel to his crew twenty years ago. He was abrupt and rude as he barked at everyone coming into his view. Rosa-Lee stayed in the background, making sure she did not attract any attention.

She followed him to the captain's cabin. He flung the D.E.I.C ensign away from him, cursing it. When his second-in-command appeared, the conversation gave it all away. She immediately ducked away into the shadows and kept quiet, listening to the angry conversation.

"Captain, did you find the man you were looking for?"

"No, dammit! It was another dead end. I will find that bastard and kill him." He gulped the contents in the glass on the table and walked away, the second following him, shutting the door behind him. They muttered angry words, words she could not understand.

Sunlight drenched the cabin, streaming in from large windows. When the men left the cabin, she stepped out of the shadows and heard a sound from the closet behind her. She went to investigate. Before she opened the door, she had her knife in her hand. A uniformed man lay inside, tied and gagged. His grey-blond hair was dishevelled, and an old wound split one cheek. Blood crusted the collar of his white shirt.

She introduced herself to him in whisper. When she removed the gag, the man said that he was the real Captain du Toit and pirates had captured the ship. She could do nothing for him. They both agreed that she must not do anything to attract their attention since they already had killed his second-in-command. She had replaced the gag after assuring him that she would do what she could to rescue him. She crept out in the empty passageway and was ready to go the main stairs when she heard footsteps forcing her to run down the next set of stairs. She then went out seeking protection in the lower deck.

She was fearful of discovery and made sure she was well hidden. Footsteps and voices filtered through the upper deck. She could do nothing but wait once again for a moment to slip away. Her situation looked bleak and at times she had to force herself not to give in to the overwhelming thoughts of anguish.

At first, she was startled when she saw Roberto unexpectedly, ready to yelp with joy, but he had knocked her unconscious before she could say anything. Now he towered above her, mad as hell, clearly not in the mood to listen.

"Did you for one moment think that I would not notice that you were gone?" came the clipped words laced with bottled up anger.

She could not answer him, too frightened of the man who spoke in a deadly tone. Her tongue still thick from the lack of water, she could only shake her head, squeaking.

"Do you want to say something?" He raised a dark brow.

She nodded her head. Enrico came into sight and offered her some water, helping her to sip it.

"You cost me two days," Roberto continued. "Because you want to be a sailor I am going to treat you like one."

"Please, Roberto, I know I am at fault, but listen. I need to tell you something," she pleaded the moment she could speak again.

"I am not interested in anything you have to say. You have placed us all in danger and I cannot let it pass without punishment." Before she could react, he barked out, "Take her to the upper deck."

"Roberto, what are you going to do?" Pierre asked fearfully.

"Teach the Señorita a lesson."

"Roberto, I hope you are not serious about doing what I think you are going to do?" and Pierre gasped in shock. He was the captain and he ran the ship as he saw fit. But this. He was taking it too far.

"Yes, exactly."

"Please, Roberto, I need to tell you something." Rosa-Lee tried again, begging as she struggles against the restrains, but he was so angry that he was not willing to listen.

"She is a woman!" Pierre yelped in disapproval. Roberto raised a dark brow in question. Pierre knew this tone. His captain was not to be dissuaded, and it would be wise to be quiet. But she was a woman. This could simply not happen.

"Who disguises herself as a man, so I will treat her as one," Roberto seethed. Rosa-Lee was afraid of the man, shivering at the coldness of his tone, not sure what he was going to do to her. By the sound of Pierre, it was something terrible.

As they marched up the steps with her body dangling between Pierre and another sailor, Rosa-Lee tried to get Pierre's attention.

"Pierre! The other ship was captured, we must help them..." Her voice broke in fear as she explained quickly.

"How do you know this?" he whispered staring at the rigid back of Captain Roberto who walked with long strides to the upper deck.

"They are looking for someone. They were determined to find this man." Her voice was thick with emotion, swallowing the cries which wanted to escape her lips. She was scared, hanging between the men like a rag doll.

Rosa-Lee knew she had to convince them, no matter what happened to her. "That is why I hid in the lower deck. It was not safe there. "She swallowed when they came in the sun, looking at Pierre with pleading eyes. "Please believe me." She struggled again against the hands that held her in iron grips.

Roberto gave the next command the moment they stepped up onto the upper deck. "Fasten her to the railing!" he barked the next order.

His men looked at him in horror. *Was their captain out of his mind?* Surely, he would not whip a woman. It was not done, never. Yet they did as they were told, fearing the captain more at this point.

"Get started." He spoke through clenched teeth, looking at the boatswain who had the whip in his hand. The man looked at him and then at Pierre with beseeching eyes. It did not matter how hard they were. This was a lady and you did not treat a lady like that.

"Are you disobeying an order, Pirate?" Roberto asked stoically, eyebrows raised, his hands on his hips. Other men moved closer, relieved they were not in the boatswain's shoes.

"Captain, I never..." The big man's voice faltered as he watched his captain walked towards Rosa-Lee.

Roberto walked over to her and ripped her shirt from her back, exposing her soft, silky skin. His heart missed a beat, but he had to continue. He had to be strong and punish her. The law of the sea requires it.

"Captain, wait. Please listen." Pierre interrupted, touching his arm. Roberto looked at him, annoyed, his face blank.

"She told me something that you need to know, Captain." He kept his voice low. He did not want to show disrespect for the man in front of the crew, but this was important.

"What is it?"

"Can we step aside? I don't want the crew to hear."

Roberto kept his eyes on her as they moved away. Another man also looked at her, the lust in his eyes visible for everyone to see, if anyone did look his way. But no one did, the play before them capturing every harden sailor. All eyes were fixated on the woman and the captain.

"Yes?" Roberto looked at him, then at Rosa-Lee, still stretched out between the ropes, her soft back exposed in the sun. She wiggled her wrists, but the ropes cut through the soft skin and red bruises formed. Roberto bit hard down on his jaw; he could not afford to be soft.

Leaning his head closer to his second-in-command, Roberto strained to hear as Pierre softly continued.

"The *Heerengardt* was captured. She did not make a distress call because the men were looking for someone else. She was hiding, hoping to get away as soon as possible. She realized she made a mistake. Roberto, you cannot flog this woman! You will have a mutiny on your hands. Look at the men."

At first, he did not want to. Seeing the worried eyes of his friend made him glance around. They barely hid their angry glares.

"Then it makes sense what we saw: no guards and only drunken men."

"Yes, Roberto. Let her go."

"Untie her!" he roared. The men sagged with relief.

The boatswain was the first to get to her, and he untied her. Roberto removed his jacket and wrapped it around her bare shoulders. As she slumped down, he caught her before she hit the deck and took her to his cabin.

9

April 05, 1625

We received a letter today that Kayla gave birth to a healthy son on October 13, 1624.

Rosa-Lee was bouncing with joy since this would make her an aunt. Chattering around the castle nonstop. It brought back memories of betrayal and the years of abuse we had to suffer under Faro. But at the end it worked out for good. I would never forget that moment when Faro admitted that Kayla was his daughter, there among every sailor and slave. Once again, I felt disgraced, but Cisco smiled at me as if he sensed my thoughts and I could not help but to let it go. But still it left a bitter taste in my mouth. Something I never talked about again.

To hear Rosa-Lee chatter about her new status made me realize how far we came and that we were still alive. Enjoying the joy of motherhood and new life.

Faro has paid for his sins.

†††

With her face hidden in his shoulder and her arms around his neck, Roberto walked down the steps to his cabin, enjoying her closeness. He did not know how she felt but he could only guess. He had humiliated her in front of pirates. What kind of a man was he?

This time his anger was aimed at himself. He held her closer to his hard body, feeling her stirring. She kept quiet, however.

Back in his cabin, he set her down in a leather chair. His eyes never left the small woman gripping the arms of the wooden arm rest. He swallowed. He did not know what to say, feeling small in her presence. When she lifted her eyes to glance at him, he could only see relief. No anger, no humiliation.

Roberto expected disgust, but for some reason she did not look at him in that manner. In a softer tone he asked, "Tell me what you have seen."

Rosa-Lee started to speak, still shaking after the ordeal. She had really thought that he was going to go through with his plan. She had never seen him so furious.

The previous day, while cooped up in the lower deck, peeping at the other pirates from her hiding place on the *Heerengardt,* she realized Roberto was in a different category from these pirates. He had integrity and honour that the others lacked. They talked about women as if they were scum. Roberto had never made her feel like that, neither him nor his crew.

She had always felt safe among them, but on the other ship, she had feared for her life, sitting quietly under the sails in the shadows of the hull. Too afraid to move, she never went outside for water or food, the risk too great to take. She was brave but on the *Heerengardt* she felt fear, out of control fear.

She could not hate Roberto. He had saved her. Even if he was angry and ready to flog her, he was still willing to listen. For that she was grateful.

Putting her feelings aside, she looked at him with relief written all over her face. The fact that he had carried her, holding her tight made her feel more than safe. She felt at home. It was a strange feeling but one she would consider later. There were more pressing issues at hand.

"When I came on board, I wanted to report you, but then I noticed the crew's strange behaviour, very peculiar for a D.E.I.C. ship. My father has met with many of those men. They all have a certain air of self-assurance about them; but this crew was eerie, scared. That I found very odd at the time. When I reached the captain's cabin, the substitute captain was fuming. When his second-in-command joined him, they talked about someone they were looking for on the *Contra O Vento,* someone that they wanted to kill. No names were mentioned, but he was very angry."

"I heard a noise in the wardrobe and when they left, I peeked inside. The real Captain Peek du Toit was tied up and gagged. When I removed the gag, he told me that pirates had captured them a week ago. The man was weak but remained calm under the distress he faced. He told me not to do something foolish and to hide. I replaced the gag and left. I was so afraid that I went and took cover in the safest place I could find. That's where you found me." Her eyes filled with hopefulness, praying that her gut was right about the pirate in front of her. His features looked sullen but still blank.

"I promised him that we would help him, Roberto," she pleaded again, taking his hands in hers, he looked down at their joined hands, and a faint grin appeared before it disappeared again. He returned his gaze to her face.

"You do know that we are pirates as well?" He stated the obvious.

"Yes, but there is such a thing as compassion and helping those in need. Those men are in need. We are the closest to help. I can only hope that somewhere in that pirate heart of yours you will see the wisdom in it. Maybe you will get one hanging less for a good deed done." She smirked.

"I like her," Pierre said with a wide-open grin.

Roberto looked at him with a glimmer of a smile but kept his voice low.

"And I suppose you have a plan?"

"No, but I am sure we can come up with something."

"You do realize that this will cause us to not meet our deadline. Your brother's life is on the line."

"My brother will understand. Please, Roberto, we need to help them." She squeezed his hand.

"We are already two days behind them, and it will cost us another day or two to catch them. Besides, we do not know in which direction they went. They could have stopped at Santiago or continued to the Mediterranean Sea."

She smirked knowingly, letting go of his hands and raising herself. "I saw the charts on the table. While they were talking, they leaned on it. When I looked at it, his fingerprint dent was still showing on the coast of Morocco. We are two days behind, but our ship is faster when we set full sails. We can make up the difference." Walking to his table, she pointed at the open chart. The men followed.

"What do you think, Pierre?"

"She's right, we can catch up the way she said."

"How many are there, besides the fake captain and his second-in-command?"

"As far as I could see, they were ten in total. There were the men that came with them on the longboat and four who guard the men on the ship," she answered.

"Give the go ahead. We are going on a rescue mission!" Roberto said to Pierre, who laughed at the new adventure. Roberto grinned, his anger forgotten.

When Pierre barked the new orders on the upper deck the pirates were stunned. Rescue mission what absurdity was this they muttered among each other but did as they were told.

†††

July 16, 1625

Will I ever forget the day I deliberately turned my back on Qonchita, the disappointment and shock when I did nothing?

It was a warm summer day like today, but there was nowhere to turn for shade. The tall grasses made it difficult to see any one. I had to make a path for the remaining group on our way to the fort. I remembered we had stopped at this fort two years ago when our supplies ran out before we could anchor in Delogao Bay farther south, down the coast.

I went to investigate and took a few men with me. They all died on the way of fever. I myself almost died as I reached the fort. The fever got hold of me, but the doctor helped me, and I lived. I was gone for three weeks. In that time the group we left behind had similar fates. Only six remained.

I recovered fully, and the governor of the fort sent a few men with me to help. With enough food and medication to assist the last survivors. It took us seven days to reach them.

We stayed for a day helping the last six to gain some strength, but it was not enough. Although tired we carried them weak and exhausted after the last encounter. I had Rosa-Lee on my back since Qonchita was too weak to even carry her own child. At one point her legs collapsed under her in pure exhaustion and we still had two days walk left. Rosa-Lee was asleep, and I decided to stop and let the people rest.

Kayla was very clingy and refused to let go of me. I wrapped both Rosa-Lee and Kayla in my arms, sat with them in my lap, and dozed off. The strain of carrying them and making a path was too much for my own weak body.

Qonchita just sat where she collapsed, bleeding, for a few hours and I left her. I didn't notice this at the time or go to her aid. When I finally woke, I looked for her fervently, and saw her crying, still at the same spot I left her. I tried to get away from the two young ones, but Kayla was determined and refused to let go. From where I sat, I could see her feet were raw once again and I turned my back. Maybe because I was so weary, nevertheless I did nothing to help her and at the end Alfonso helped her.

As sick as he was, he administered the ointment I had brought with me from the fort, applying it to her feet. She was angry with me and did not talk to me while we walked to the fort. Even during the first week of our recovery at the fort she kept her distance.

In the end, fear of a spider caused her to run back to me. When I "rescued" her and carried her away in my arms, I explained as best I could. She is beautiful when angry. I had great pleasure watching her as she went on about it, but when I kissed her into silence she was like putty in my hands.

She forgave me.

10

Enrico and Pierre left them alone and a silence fell between them. Rosa-Lee, still shaky of hunger, sat down in the Captain's chair, not realizing that such a thing was never done.

The past few days' experience had left her numb. The moment she stepped on that ship she knew she was wrong and even deserved the whipping, yet she was thankful that they did not follow through with it.

Her father had told her on many occasions that the life of a sailor was very hard, and the Captain's discipline was important to run a ship sufficiently. Whether it was a D.E.I.C. or pirate ship, discipline was the only thing a captain had to keep the men in check, upholding his law always.

Finally, she spoke, "I am sorry for the delay that I caused." She looked down at her hands in her lap.

Roberto walked closer to her. Kneeling in front of her, he softly said: "I was never so scared in my whole life because of what you did. I was afraid that I would not see you again. I was angry, frustrated, not knowing if you would be all right. Angry for the situation we were in and that I could not change it." The seriousness of the situation was visible on his face and Rosa-Lee had to swallow hard at the lump in her throat.

"Does this mean that I am forgiven?" Rosa-Lee asked softly.

"Never do this again!" he said brusquely. He could not believe how vulnerable he was before her, kneeling in front of her. He wanted to pull her closer, his body aching for her warmth next to him.

Their faces were so close that he could lean in and touch those rosebud lips. Amazed at the tenderness and care in him, reflected by her own, Rosa-Lee absently brought her hand up and trailed the scar on his face with one finger.

"Tell me the story," she whispered.

"Not much to tell. It was a long time ago. I killed a man who raped my sister. This was his reminder to me." He also spoke in a soft husky tone. When her finger ended at his lips, he kissed it.

"It is a beautiful scar." She pressed her forehead against his, his closeness affecting her. Her body yearned for his touch. For the moment all was forgotten. He kissed her fingers and then her palm, removing it and placing a kiss on her mouth.

"You do things to me that I have never experienced," she finally said, leaning back. "And I think I need to go. This can never be." Pushing him aside, she stood up. His hands brushed over her curves and his jacket fell to the ground. She walked out, exposing creamy skin with each step.

Her presence lingered in the cabin for a few seconds and when he gathered his jacket from the floor; he could smell her on it. Deep in thought, he slipped into it, her warmth captured inside. He breathed her in.

What was that all about? He had never knelt before a woman, let alone told anyone the story of his scar. Never had he felt this vulnerable in all his life. He thought she merely intrigued him.

114

But he found it was more than just attraction or thoughts of a few minutes rolling in the hay.

He had feelings for her.

He knew she had the same struggles as he did. Her feelings for him were crystal clear for that brief second when she touched his cheek, trailing her small finger down his cheek and letting it stop at his lips.

She was fighting, refusing to recognize it.

Smiling softly, he thought he would have to be patient with her. He could understand why she was fighting it. In her eyes, he was a pirate. Ladies like her never fell in love with pirates. It was unheard of. His life foretold an unsavoury future, a life no woman would be willing to share. But then, he was not an ordinary pirate. He could have a future with her, but he could not reveal it. Not now.

He could still feel her touch on his face. He enjoyed the memory of the delicate caress against the scar, emotions she stirred; what it did to him. Sitting down on the chair she had left, he leaned back and closed his eyes, a smile on his handsome face.

†††

"Captain, we have set the sails and we are on our way to the *Heerengardt*. The winds look good," Pierre reported after a while.

"That is good."

Roberto stood over the maps and studied them, but Pierre knew him. His thoughts were not with the maps. His guess would be that they were with the beautiful señorita.

He had seen how Roberto looked at her when he thought nobody was watching. His captain was in love with her, and who could blame him? She was not only beautiful but very intelligent too. She was a novelty in these times where women were only expected to have children and do household chores, staying in the background.

The Señorita could speak to them about things that interested them. She had a sharp mind. She had proven it again with her perception about the *Heerengardt*. If he had half a chance, he would pursue her. His captain would not like the competition.

†††

A while later Rosa-Lee came on deck. She wore a beautiful pale green dress, her skin glowing and hair shiny, looking magnificent. She was the picture of a stunning female, now more than before.

Roberto watched her from the bridge as she stood at the railing, peering over the waters in the direction of the captive ship. They were going at a good speed. The winds had picked up and the ship cleaved the water, leaving a white trail behind.

"At this rate we will catch up in time," Roberto thought.

The stormy weather they had experienced the previous evening had fled but left them with a good strong wind blowing the sails in a sharp convex. The wooden beams creaked under its force.

The meal bell reverberated through the ship and he walked down the steps off the bridge. He met Rosa-Lee at the bottom and offered his arm to walk her to the dining hall. With a smile, she gladly accepted, placing a small hand on the sleeve of his jacket. He inhaled. She smelled like cinnamon and honey, his favorite scents.

"Are you feeling better?" He inquired.

"Yes, thank you. The bath was wonderful, and Enrico is very good."

"I am glad you are pleased, Mon Petite." He let the endearing words slip and she smiled, looking down at her feet, the stairs steep in front of her.

Once they were seated, Pierre asked, "What is the plan of action?"

"I have given it much thought," Rosa-Lee said immediately, and both Roberto and Pierre grinned at the señorita's self-assuredness. This they had to hear. The other men looked dumb-founded at the three.

"The moment that we are close enough to send a signal, we will send a distress call. I, as a diversion, will go on board while you --" looking at both Pierre and Roberto "-- Will come from behind and free the captain and his crew. Easy." She shrugged her shoulders casually. Roberto thought his heart almost stopped at the ridiculous plan.

"There is no way that I will allow you to go on that ship again," said Roberto abruptly, glaring at her.

"Now wait, Roberto. That sounds like a great plan."

"No."

"Do you have a better idea?" Pierre asked with a grin. His friend was smitten.

"Please, Captain, we can help these men and I can make a better diversion than you can. My life will be safe. I mean, I am surrounded with D.E.I.C. men. There are only ten pirates. We can take them out." Her logic was too simple for him. How could he put her back, knowing what he had just discovered?

All eyes were on him, the food forgotten, as they waited.

Debating with himself, weighing both the pros and cons, he knew this was the best plan. Reluctantly, Roberto had to agree to the plan and finally said:

"I agree. It can work, but if there is, at any time, the smallest notion that your life is in danger, we pull out. Is that clear?"

"Yes, clear." both Pierre and Rosa-Lee agreed, and they smiled to each other.

"Let's eat," said Rosa-Lee. "I am starving." Chuckles filled the cabin; even Roberto revealed a grin before it disappeared again.

11

Watching the woman eating, Roberto could not believe he just agreed to this insane plan. His mind raced, trying to find a new plan, but hers was the best. He admitted after a few minutes. She clearly had put a lot of thought into it and they could win. Setting the captain and his men free for a get out of jail free card… he smirked.

The whole idea was preposterous but as he watched her it grew on him just as she grew on him. He knew he had feelings for her but to what extent he did not want to admit. But she brought out the best in him. She was more than he expected and in only a short time he could not imagine giving her to the Falcon. That was a thought that kept him awake often.

The whole idea of putting her in danger among the other pirates made his palms sweaty. His heart throbbed. So many things could go wrong. And he would never forgive himself if she got hurt.

He watched as she listened to the conversation at the table, smiling sweetly at the men, and another emotion surged through him. One he had never encountered before.

He frowned as she talked to Pierre, who listened to her with interest. When Pierre looked at him, Roberto scowled. His second smiled and continued with the conversation. Her laughter rang through the air. It annoyed him, and he pushed his chair away, stepping out into the passageway as the door slammed behind him.

He knew he was acting childlike, but he could not help himself. He walked to his cabin and plopped down in the chair. Thoughts rushed through him. *Come on, man. The woman can talk to whomever she wants. She is not married to you.* He squirmed in his chair. Seeing a glass of wine on his desk he took one huge swig and smacked his lips as the red liquid poured down his throat. His thoughts stuck on the word *married.* As if something had struck him, he briskly walked out of his cabin to the upper deck, knowing that his thoughts would be best occupied when busy.

It took them eighteen hours to catch up with the *Heerengardt* near the north coast of Morocco, at the curve where the Atlantic and the Mediterranean met. It was already late, and Roberto decided to do it early in the morning, when most of those men would still be asleep. He was hoping they would have a good run-in with the rum barrel the previous evening.

They chose a few trusted men to go with them and brought them up to speed with the plan. All of them were eager to help the fellow sailors, even if they were technically enemies.

Just as the sun broke over the horizon the *Contra O Vento* sent a distress signal and the *Heerengardt* answered. The long boat had left an hour earlier with the chosen men on their way to the other side of the ship, waiting for the signal from Roberto.

The longboat had lowered onto the water and Rosa-Lee was let down with Fausto who accompanied her. The Spaniard's short, bulky frame concealed his strength and speed, both with weapons and his fists. He was the only man Roberto trusted to protect her at all costs.

Roberto thought his heart was going to stop at the sight of her. To think that he gave in to the plan was utter madness.

He swallowed at the lump in his throat, followed Pierre into the water, and swam behind the longboat to get unnoticed to the *Heerengardt*. They would then continue around the ship where they would meet the other men and get up with a rope fastened to their waists.

They were both masked, their identities sealed from prying people. They were still pirating, enemies on the waters. As they approached the ship, Rosa-Lee made sure that her dress revealed enough to keep the "captain" busy. Roberto almost had a heart attack when he saw her at first. Her bosom was showing too much soft roundness for his taste, and her small waist was even more accentuated. Some of his men smiled with pleasure and he gave them angry warning looks.

To display her attributes before other men was not good at all. It made him resentful to the whole absurd idea all over again. And again, that unknown feeling coursed through him. It was an emotion so new to him that he did not recognize it at first, until Pierre pointed it out and Roberto told him to shut his mouth. The man was pleased with the discovery of Roberto's envious emotions and gleeful, full of mischievous behaviour. Roberto knew he would never hear the end of this.

Rosa-Lee made sure that the men on the *Heerengardt's* eyes were glued on her so that they would not notice the two men behind them. The boatswain had warned her a few times to take it easy, not to fall over the side, at which she just shrugged her shoulders and continued, enjoying the adventure. However, she was nervous and did not want to show it to Roberto. She was hiding behind the bravado. To show so much of herself was a first. She had never flaunted herself deliberately and felt self-conscious about it, but the reaction from Roberto surprised her in a good way.

When she finally got on board, the impostor greeted her keenly. He seemed ugly as his eyes ran hungrily over her body. She had to fight the shivers running through her.

She swallowed at the bile threatening to rise and plastered a smile on her face.

This is what she was aiming for. Distraction.

"My good captain, finally we can meet. I was distracted when you were on the ship earlier. Your fame precedes you, and your second in command is a worthy opponent." This caused the bald man to grin pridefully and he received a stern look from the imposter. Rosa-Lee just stopped herself in time when a giggle wanted to erupt and continued. "When I was in distress, I convinced the men to bring me here. That captain, Roberto, what a beast!" She rolled her eyes in disdain, sighed heavily at the mere thought, and touched her heart, "Not a gentleman at all. I could not stay there any longer. His hands were always groping. Not a way to treat a lady," she added for effect, smiling sweetly at the ugly man whose lingering snakelike gaze was on her ample cleavage. Her hand fell at her side in mock-surrender.

"Señorita, it is an honour to meet you! You can be sure that we will take good care of you. That captain did look like a beast to me," he agreed, smacking his lips, his eyes barely meeting her own as he once again fixed them on her chest.

Roberto had just come over the railing when he heard the comment and blew through his nose in disgust.

"What an insult!" he thought his face in a scowl. He glanced at Rosa-Lee briefly, convinced that she was safe and sound. He noticed the men surrounding her. One tried to touch her, and he balled his fists. It was all an act, he knew, but still. *Did she have to make it look so good?* he thought angrily.

He signed to Pierre that the coast was clear and turned to keep watch as he and the rest of the men followed. Each man knew what to do. Stealthily they all moved and separated.

They both slipped into the castle, where the captain's cabin would be. The remaining men went down the stairs to free the crew. Rosa-Lee strolled with the pirates in the opposite direction, laughing at the joke she just heard, touching the captain's arm ever so delicately.

Fixated with her, they hardly took note of anything else around them as she told them a story, fluttering her eyelashes provocatively.

Rosa-Lee could not believe that she could act so tartly. The men were drooling over her and she doubt they heard a word she said but she had to keep them occupied until Roberto rescued the men. Their bodily odours wafting in her nose and she took deep breaths as she placed her hand delicately before her nose.

Her heart pounded in her chest and she was sure one would notice the rapid beat, but her cleavage was of greater concern to them. One tried to touch her, but she slapped him playfully and chuckled when he took his hand away sheepishly.

Please hurry, Roberto. Her lips tightened into a smile even though she felt uncomfortable among them.

Several minutes later, the voice of the real captain roared over the deck. Scuffles broke out all around them. Rosa-Lee was pushed aside and against the railings and she watched as the ten pirates were captured almost simultaneously. The whole takeover happened swiftly, without any sound of a drawn sword, and Rosa-Lee had to admit that Roberto was superb.

She could not help but to admire him as he stood there, tall dark and proud. His eyes the only muscle that moved, the rest of his face covered behind the bandana and his hat pushed low over his face. She wanted to run to him, but futility stopped her. If the D.E.I.C captain new who his saviors were they too would be apprehended. The feeling of relief and wonder captured in her heart and she knew once back on the other ship she had to think about this.

Held in steel grips, the pirates could not fight back. The leader was in noticeable distress but said nothing as the real Captain, Peek du Toit, just stared him down. The impressive figure of the older man was intimidating to the impostors and allowed no rebuff.

The D.E.I.C crew took control, surrounding the men with no way of escape. They were taken down below, where they would be tried and immediately hung.

There was no mercy for pirates.

"I have to thank you, Señorita, that you came back to help us," Captain du Toit said after the deck was once again under his command. Sailors scattered around as they started to do their daily chorus. "I remember your voice. It was so quick that I thought I was dreaming, but here you are! For eight days I was a captive in that dresser with no way of escape. Why were you on my ship in the first place?" The captain asked in all sincerity. Pierre and Roberto who stood silently in the shadows drew in their breaths, waiting for her reply.

"There was a huge misunderstanding on my part about the *Contra O Vento*, and I fled from the ship in a typical lady-like fit." She chuckled with delight. "The captain set me straight quickly after he rescued me. I must admit, I was more afraid on board your ship than on the *Contra O Vento*."

"Señorita, we owe you our gratitude! Is there anything that we can do for you?"

"If you can deliver this letter to the D.E.I.C, it would be appreciated." Roberto had passed her a letter that morning just before she descended the Jacob ladder and she gave it to the captain. At the time, she thought it was odd for a pirate to ask this request, without any explanation. The look he gave her was one of *Trust me,* and he gave her a rueful smile. Her heart raced but she nodded her head in acceptance and placed it in her skirt pocket.

More things to add to the already confusing puzzle in her mind and heart. She was falling for the pirate. In just a few short days her heart was pulling toward the rogue. No matter how she tried she could not ignore the feelings he stirred.

"Can I ask who you are?" the captain requested. Nervously she looked in the direction of Roberto who was still covered by the shadows and he nodded, the mask still covering his identity.

She laughed softly. "I am so sorry, my good captain, my manners are unforgivable. If my mama could see me now…" and she chuckled, the captain grinned sheepishly.

His glance at her bosom irritated Roberto but he could not fault the man. It was enticing. As he witnessed the conversation, making sure that he was not too obvious to the crew of the *Heerengardt,* he could not help but admire the woman. Pierre touched his arm, which drew his attention away to a tall soldier walking directly to them. He knew it was time to leave.

While she introduced herself to the captain the two dark figures moved over the tackle work, down the steps and hid in the corner. Footsteps stopped just above their heads and then followed down the steps as well. Both men held their breath. When the man stood still and looked down the passageway they waited. Pierre's hand was almost touching the soldier's hat. A few seconds passed that felt like minutes. Then he disappeared up the steps and they breathed again. Both knew it was time to get out of there before the man got it in his head to sound the alarm.

"I am Rosa-Lee Almaida."

"The daughter of Cisco Almaida?" he asked, meeting her eyes.

"Yes," she nodded.

"What an honour! I have heard so much about your father." He clapped his hands together in appreciation.

"Thank you, Captain." She smiled sweetly up at him, keeping the Captain's attention as the two figures emerged on deck and slipped over the railing in record time.

"Well, we need to be on our way," Rosa-Lee said. "Please make sure that you deliver the letter. It is of the utmost importance."

"Yes, I will. We will be there in a month's time, and then I will hand it to them."

"Thank you, Captain. Good-bye, and a safe journey to you."

"You too, Señorita."

They helped her back into the longboat where Fausto waited for her, Pierre and Roberto were in the water invisible to the men on the ship. The rest of the *Contra's* crew had already left. Shattered nerves amongst the soldiers on the *Heerengardt* might have sparked outrage at every unfamiliar face they set their eyes on. The rescuers thought it wise to withdraw quickly.

Rosa-Lee smiled as she sat down, her hand in Fausto's as he helped her to take a seat. Her dress puffed all around her. Clouded in green taffeta it emphasised the beauty with in.

Proudly she sat in the long boat, shoulders straight, as Fausto took the oars and started to row away from the ship. She smiled and waved at the men on the ship and thought: *There was no real danger in this adventure.* She held both the sides of the boat, peering over the waters with a small smile.

Roberto looked at her with curiosity. From his place in the water he could not help but to admire her. She surprised him almost every day, and there was not a scared bone in her body. She intrigued him more and more.

"Life will definitely not be boring with her around," he thought as he smiled, his eyes lingering on her enticing bosom.

12

After their daring undertaking, they returned safely from the *Heerengardt* and were back to their normal routine, on the way to the Falcon with much lost time to make up.

Roberto reminded Rosa-Lee that if anything of that sort happened again, she would face a severe flogging without hesitation. She had to confess that she was more afraid of Roberto now, after he had rescued her. His dark eyes had menacingly reinforced to her his stern warning. Even more than remembering those brutes she was among on the *Heerengardt,* her heart still stopped when thoughts of the previous day entered her mind. Thoughts that Roberto was serious when he had fastened her to the railing threw her heart into turmoil.

She had trembled so much from shock that she did not even feel ashamed of her exposure in front of the crew. Her brother's shirt had covered her chest and only her back had been bared.

To be so close to a flogging would make her think twice before another attempt. Rosa-Lee realized that although abducted and prisoner of Roberto she had nothing to fear from him except if she crossed him.

This man might like her. She had seen the looks of interest on his face, but he was still a pirate, the son of the Falcon; a fierce and cruel man.

Respect and discipline were of the utmost importance.

She had a lot of time for herself and spent most of it on the upper deck reading or walking. The cabin was too confining and small for her to breathe properly. She liked to watch them all working on the deck, repairing and cleaning the sails and all the tackle, keeping the ship well-maintained.

Most times, she would study the man Roberto from underneath her lashes as she continued with her needlework or reading. She admired the way his men respected him, obeying his instructions to the smallest detail. Though maybe they did it out of fear most times, she sensed a genuine respect toward him. He was not afraid of doing the small, mundane stuff with them. She loved the way he laughed without any care, interacting with them on competition days, climbing like rats into the ropes to see who would be first. His strength and fitness attracted her so that she openly stared at him.

During their off times, the crew would ask her to tell another story and she gladly accommodated them.

On one occasion she saw Roberto's strictness with a man who was lazy on the job, but he still managed to be kind to him. It reminded her of a story that had made a huge impression on her young mind. When everyone was settled around her she told them what she had witnessed.

"The captain that led us was a cruel man. He was always seeking for ways of making life difficult for the crew, especially my father, the big giant," she smiled, missing the man who played such a big role in her growing-up years.

"When I first saw that man after we came aboard in India, I, at the tender age of four, ran to him and gave him a huge hug. First, he looked lonely and sad and that attracted me to him. Secondly, his whole posture was one that promised safety. At first, he didn't want to speak to me, shooing me away, but he couldn't resist my childish charm." She chuckled while the men grinned.

"I continued speaking to him because, in my young heart, I was desperate for a father's touch. However, without me knowing it, I put him in danger. At first, the captain said it was acceptable because my mother was upset. When she overheard another sailor saying that he would be flogged, she pleaded on Cisco's behalf, but as I already said, the captain was a cruel man." Sadness shadowed her eyes.

"The next morning, he was tied to the ropes and flogged. Ten lashes because he answered a few questions! My mother tried to hide it from me, but I did see it. My young heart was aching for the big man and I ran away and cried where she could not see me." She dabbed away the moisture from her eyes and continued.

"After the storm and the shipwreck, we landed on a strip of white sand. While on land, people became sick or were so tired of the long walk that they just lay down in defeat. The captain refused to take care of them and left them behind. Sometimes you could hear the screams of these people as wild animals attacked and killed them. He would laugh about it. It would anger Cisco, but he kept quiet, his back still painful after another lashing because he had saved my mother; had saved all of us. Food was very scarce. The giant wanted to go out and hunt, but the captain refused to give them any ammunition. It was more precious than gold at that time and as he said, he was not going to waste good bullets on animals. Some literally starved to death. We had only the plants around us to eat. We ate leaves and bark, but some would become so sick from cramps with the unnatural diet, that they were left behind to die by the cruelty of the animals we could hear all around us."

Roberto sat close by and listened, watching her as she relived those days, all the men's attention on her.

"I remember one day we came across an empty village and they searched around to gather some food. Suddenly shots broke the silence and we saw the captain looking frantically around and shooting blindly into the thick bushes. When my mother and father went to investigate, they found a young pregnant woman killed. They were devastated at the cruelty of this man, but they could do nothing to prevent this senseless killing. After that, he found stray dogs, grilled them and forced us to eat. My mother refused, and father went back to the village later that night looking for food, which he found and brought to us."

"This man, our captain, finally died after he himself became mad with the fever that killed most of the group. He wanted to kill Father in his delirious state. Out of self-defence, Father had to kill him." She closed her eyes, the images still so clear in her mind.

"My father took over the role of captain and life became easier. The people had a great respect for him. Under his leadership no one was left behind. No one was hungry if he could prevent it."

She had to brush a tear away, missing both of her parents extremely.

"Tell us another one. How were you saved?" one of the men asked. Silence ruled on the ship as men listened to her. A few could tell their own stories of that hard-savage country, but it was nicer to listen to the young woman. Her voice was soothing to their hardened hearts.

"Father had to leave us at one stage. The group was very tired and weak from weeks without any nutrition. Food was very scarce, so he decided to go ahead and explore the land closer to the coast. By his calculations, we had to be close to a fort. Mozambique was still far off. If he could get a ship at the fort, it could take us to Mozambique and bring everyone to safety quicker. He left another sailor, who was, and still is, a very good friend, in charge of the group. Before he left, he set some traps, in the hopes that small animals could be caught to prepare as meals."

"He was gone for four weeks. We later found out that the search party, consisting of thirteen men, all came down with fever and ten died on the way. When they reached the fort, my father himself became very sick. After he regained his health, he arranged for a ship that was willing to wait for us and came back with enough food. By the time, my father finally returned with the necessary food supply, we were all literally at the doorstep of death. The fever plagued our group as well and one by one, people died. My mother and half-sister were the only two able to stand, but they were exhausted in caring for everyone. My mother became so thin that father did not recognize her at first, and when he did, he cried uncontrollably."

She closed her eyes, seeing her mother's skeletal figure with pale blue skin stretched thinly over it. The image imprinted in her mind.

"It was painful to see them in that state. At that point, they did not care that my biological father was still around. They just held each other, longing for the comfort that they could only find with each other. After he buried the dead and rested, Father took us back, carrying me on his back. Five days later, we were at the fort. The fort's occupants helped us to get enough rest and decent food and water to sustain us, so we could go onto the ship. Two days later, another storm hit us and once again, we had to abandon the ship. My biological father died during that storm. He threw himself from the ship into the whirlpool of angry waters, knowing he was losing his mind."

She swallowed again at the memories of that man. She could not even remember what he looked like anymore.

"His way of life finally caught up with him. The captain of the fort helped us again and for a full week, we could rest and have decent food. After losing the others, father decided that he needed to go to Mozambique to get help. He meant to travel alone on foot. The group decided they would go with him and not stay behind. My mother was the first to refuse to let him go alone. She did not want to be apart from him any longer. We all walked along the coast line until we reached Mozambique a week later, this time without any difficulties. The governor was good to us and helped us to get on our feet again. Regaining our strength with a great deal of rest and well-balanced meals made the world of difference. Another month passed by before a ship passed that was willing to take us back to Portugal."

"How long did it take you to get back?" another sailor asked.

"Two years in total since we left India and reached Portugal," She replied.

"Will you ever go back there?"

"Never. The memories still haunt me. My mother and father took great care in helping me forget, but I have learnt to take it day by day. Mostly the faces of those people that stayed behind in fear and trembling haunt me. I didn't fear the savages so much as the cruelty of the captain to my father. It was very real. When the ship went down the first time and we reached the shore father built a hut for us because we did not know how long we would stay there. The captain hoped that another ship would pass but after a week it did not happen, and the food was already scarce. The search teams stayed away for longer and longer times.

My biological father decided he was going to stay in our hut while we were on the beach. My mother refused but he tried to overpower her. Father stepped in when he heard her scream for help and saved her. He received a flogging because of that from the captain. Those are the things that I struggle with the most."

"Why do you say that your biological father wanted to rape your mother? Weren't they married?" the men asked in confusion.

"Yes, they were, but my mother was forced into the marriage by her parents. On their wedding night he forced himself on her and nine months later I was born. My mother never forgave him for that, and she never allowed him to touch her again. When he saw that there were feelings between the sailor and my mother, he was jealous and wanted to try again; again, with the same brutality."

For the hardened pirates it was difficult to comprehend. They were used to taking what they wanted, even by force, but when injustice was done by the rich, they could not fathom it. Those were the people who dictated how they all should live, yet they still can do such cruelties to their own.

There is no honour in that.

13

Another week passed before a storm hit them. Heavy rains fell like buckets from the sky onto them and the strong winds blew them around like a feather on the ocean. Rosa-Lee had to tie ropes around herself to stay on top of the deck, trying very hard not to panic as the water crashed over them. Pierre tried several times to convince her to go below deck but she refused. The stifling cabin would not become her coffin. When the first heavy rain fell, she came topside, even though fear gripped her thoughts. She stayed in the middle as men scattered around her to tie the equipment to the rails. Bravely she watched as the waves pounded down on them, Roberto barking orders through the thunderous clouds. He could barely hear his voice as a whisper, but it did not stop the men from doing their work. When the pounding became uncontrollable, she decided to tie herself down.

Waves higher than the ship fell on them all with crushing strength. Men rushed over the deck as water ran like strong currents over the rolling deck. Everyone was drenched, tired and cold but they could not slacken and during this time after another brutal crash Rosa-Lee was swept into the ocean. The rope and a part of the ship's railing were still tied around her. Shock and fear gripped her heart the moment she plunged into the dark angry depths. She tried desperately to untangle herself, but it was futile. Her chest burned and with one last desperate attempt she reached out her hand to be pulled back in, losing all consciousness.

"Man overboard!" The cry went out from the crowmaster. Roberto rushed over to see who it was. His heart raced as Alexi yelled that it was Rosa-Lee. Without any thought, he tied a rope around his waist and dove into the whirlpool of dark waters.

Praying to God above to save her as the dark waters covered his body. Franticly he searched the darkness for the fragile body.

With the first few attempts, he could not find her. It was pitch black as waves continue to crash down over him, burning his eyes and lungs. Desperately he kicked around him.

From the ship, men brought lanterns closer and as the glimmer of the light fell on the dark waters. He finally saw her pale blue dress bobbing in the swells, her head disappearing at an alarming rate into the dark depths. He had to go after her. Her dress was too heavy for her to stay afloat on the water. Kicking with everything he had within him, he followed the lifeless body.

When he reached her, he pulled the rope, indicating that they could pull them up. Steadily the sailors pulled them in. Waves crashing over them without any attention to stop.

Breaking through the water's surface he sucked in huge gulps of air as more water broke over them. He swallowed mouthfuls of the salty water, coughing but never let go of his cargo.

Finally, they reached safety on the rolling deck. Men grabbed and hoisted them over the railing. Getting his footing, Roberto laid the lifeless body down. He pounded on her back out of desperation to get the water out her lungs and much needed air in. Her face was a grey-blue and water dripped down her bruised face. He brushed her hair away, trying to do whatever he could to get her to live, even slapping her face but nothing happened.

He called out her name in desperation. Cold and lifeless, she lay in front of him, and he thought his life was over.

The ropes around her had cut into her flesh which he had to cut them away. The flesh on her shoulder was slashed open where she had scraped against wood and nails, covering the normally creamy skin in red blood. She looked terrible. Roberto panicked for the first time in his life, the storm forgotten, as he was fixated on her.

He called for the doctor while gripping her body to him, slapping her face and whispering how much he loved her. Everything happened so fast, the roaring sounds of the storm vanishing as his heart pounded in his chest.

He loved her. The concept emerged within his heart and he had no time to tell her. But there was no time to ponder this new revelation.

She was lifeless and pale grey. The doctor rushed to her side and pushed him away. Tilting her neck, he quickly gave her mouth to mouth; working with her. Finally, she gave that one desperate gasp for air, coughing up water. It run from her mouth and nose and breathing in the life-giving oxygen.

Roberto was so relieved that he grabbed her body in a fierce embrace, kissing the ice-cold face with desperate kisses. Over the past few weeks, he really had started to care for her and when the true reflection of his heart shimmered through, he did not care who saw him. He wanted to tell her, his face adorned in a smile amid the still-raging storm.

"You are hurting me," she coughed out, and the doctor grinned.

"Apologies señorita," He replied in a whisper, almost reverently. A small smile touched her lips before she fell into an exhausted sleep. Shocked, he looked at the doctor, but he squeezed his shoulder.

"It is all right. She will be fine. Take her to her cabin." He commanded. With ease Roberto lifted her in his arms and carried her to her cabin. He brushed soft kisses over her face, his heart too big for his chest. When he placed her on the bed, he thought she was the most stunning woman he had ever met.

Rosa-Lee Almaida looked fragile and small, but he did not see that. He only saw her beauty gripping his heart.

The markings of the rope on her shoulder were red and swollen. Her dress was torn, and they knew they would have to get it off and as he held her, peeling the wet, torn fabric from her body, he could not help but to look at her, appreciating the curves in front of him. The good doctor spoke sternly, and he let her down, covering the body with a blanket.

"We will have to hope that she does not get an infection in that shoulder. Step aside, please." he commanded again. After closer inspection he found a broken nail imbedded in her shoulder.

Roberto brought a light closer while the doctor searched in his bag. Founding what he was looking for; he pulled tweezers out. He then dipped into the bag again to come out with a bottle of spirits. He dipped the tweezers in it and proceed to pull the nail effortlessly out. She flinched, still unconscious.

Blood streamed from her shoulder and Roberto gasped softly. He watched as the doctor worked on her. He put a few stitches in the shoulder and bandaged it with a white cloth. The rest of the bruises and cuts he disinfected and placed a powder on them before he closed them as well. Her face was bruised and swollen but the doctor assured him that would go away. The cuts would not become permanent scars and for that, he was grateful.

That whole night, despite Roberto's tiredness, he sat with her after the doctor left. Pierre brought him some dry clothes and he towelled himself down changing into the dry clothes. Slumping into the chair next to her bed. The storm calmed down about an hour later.

When he finally woke the sun was streaming into the cabin and she was looking at him, smiling.

What a welcome sight.

"I owe you thanks for saving me." Her voice was still rough from the near-drowning.

"Can I give you some water?" he asked as he came closer, squinting his eyes. They were still burning from the salt water.

"Yes, please. I believe the storm has calmed down. Is there much damage to the ship?"

"It is manageable. Nothing that we cannot repair."

He smiled back, his heart racing at her smile. The paleness had made way for colour and she looked beautiful against the white sheets. Her dark hair was dry and dishevelled, but that made her more appealing to him.

"How do you feel?"

"Tired, stiff and aching all over my body, but happy to be alive. I remember you dove into the waters to rescue me. You are a real hero. How will I ever repay you?"

"By allowing me to love you," he said without thought. She looked at him in wonder, this man that she was trying very hard to understand.

He loved her. A pirate had fallen in love with her. *How was this possible?*

"I still hate you for what you have done to me and my parents."

"I know. However, it does not change the fact that I have feelings for you. Last night confirmed it. For me, there will be no one else but you," he said with conviction as he came closer and knelt before her, his eyes trained on her with all the emotions he felt. He wanted her to see it. He wanted to convince her as he took her hand and brought it to his lips.

She was stunned at his confession and had no reply as she saw the tenderness in his eyes. Love was prominent in the ochre depths, and she stared back into those depths, her future brightly shining as he opened his heart. Her heart raced as she struggled to sit up, forgetting the pain of her body. She was just bathing in his revelation. The hate that she felt for him had melted away and in its place, love shone in the depths of her own eyes. She touched his cheek, tracing the scar once again and when her finger stopped at the corner of his lips, he kissed it.

"Please let me love you," he whispered before his lips touched her lips. She closed her eyes, just revelling in his touch, his tenderness. Her heart sped up another notch. Softly she sighed and leaned into him. He captured her mouth with a desperate plea, until he pulled her closer and she flinched in pain. Withdrawing, he laid her down, the love shining unmistakable, and she smiled.

"You need to give me some time. This is very confusing to me," she finally said. "I find your company pleasant and not once did I feel afraid while with you. You always treat me with respect, and I admire you for the captain you are. However, this does not change the fact that you are a pirate and that I am the price of a sick scheme."

He stood up and sat next to her on the bed, taking her other hand, clutching the two together in his warm hands and said,

"Not everything is as it seems."

"What do you mean?" she asked, looking up to him, eyes wide.

"I am going to ask you to trust me. I will never hurt you intentionally. There are many things happening in the background that I cannot tell you about, but if you can trust me, it will be a great start. Love will come. You are not indifferent to me, and that much I know." He kissed her hands for a second time. Her fingers tingled under his touch.

Again, she looked at him, perplexed, allowing herself to enjoy the kiss. His voice was soft and soothing. Again, she reached out, touching the scar on his face. It made him even more attractive to her. Her eyes showed her heart and he leaned over, brushing his lips over her face. She closed her eyes, enjoying the closeness of him, her heart racing. When he lifted his head he said softly,

"I love you, Rosa-Lee Almaida." She smiled, her body trembling with exhaustion and excitement. She relaxed into the softness of the mattress. He could see that her eyes wanted to close. Her tiredness was still evident on her. He bent over, placing again a kiss on her forehead and said,

"I will leave for a while so that you can sleep. Later I will be back with food. You need to eat. There is something we need to discuss." She nodded and dozed off into a deep sleep, a soft smile on the beautiful face. He smiled, stroking the bluish cheek before he walked out of her cabin. The smile on his face reflected his heart. He covered a yawn as he entered his own cabin.

He was tired to the bone.

†††

Several hours later, awakened by the most delicious smells filling her cabin, she opened her eyes. When she tried to move, pain shot up into her shoulder and she moaned. Roberto rushed over to her.

"Are you all right, my Rosa?"

"My shoulder hurts," she said hoarsely.

"The doctor said your shoulder looks much better and there is no sign of infection, but it will take a while to heal. The nails did do some damage on your shoulder," he explained.

"Thanks, Roberto, for taking such good care of me." She smiled again. "A lady can get use to this." He bent over and kissed her.

This was not a dream. She thought she had dreamt all of it but now that he repeated the words and showed it by taking care of her, she knew it had to be true.

"I would love to take care of you always," he said softly, his eyes darker than normal, his breath warm against her skin. She leaned forward and kissed him softly.

"See, there is hope for me," he chuckled, helping her to sit up, draping a robe over her naked shoulders and brushing against the soft skin. Their eyes locked. The blush that appeared on her face was the most appealing thing he had ever seen. He smiled. "Beautiful." He cupped the bruised face. "I love you."

"I thought it was a dream." Her eyes wide in wonder

"No dream, my Rosa." And he kissed her on the cheek "This is real. I have to admit it caught me off guard but once I accepted the feeling, I could not keep it for myself." He touched her cheek softly. "Do you believe me?"

Sheepishly she nodded her head as she stared up to him, her heart racing but her mind still in turmoil. "Yes, I believe you," she finally said, and he grinned.

Walking to the table, he brought the food over and helped her to eat. She was not as tired anymore and they could talk a few minutes before Pierre called him away to attend to a matter on the upper deck.

Later, after the doctor visited, she dozed off in a restful sleep. Once she was awake again Enrico helped her with her hair, washing it carefully which she appreciated. Every person on the ship was doting on her and she could not help but soften her

144

heart, a little bit. When hot water was carried in, she had no words. Their care touched her heart. Thoughtful of the changes since the pirate declared his love to her. It was if the entire ship had changed.

The moment she was left alone, she lay in the warm bath, careful not to dampen the bandaged shoulder, soaking the stiffness away. Her body stung, but it felt good to be clean again.

Looking at her own reflection in the small handheld mirror, afterwards she looked at her face. Swelling and bruises covered her face and briefly she thought about scars. Her beauty was something she appreciated but was not obsessed about it. Now her normal reflection showed another side. Could she live with that if permanent?

When Enrico entered her cabin and saw what she was doing he spoke softly, "You still look beautiful, señorita." And she smiled faintly. It will not help to dwell on it, she thought as she placed the mirror down. The rest of the afternoon she thought about Roberto and his feelings for her. He asked her to trust him and she knew she did trust him. Not sure when it had changed but she felt safe amongst him and the men. But would that be love, to respond to the love she could clearly see in his own eyes?

He said he wanted to discuss something, and he was quite serious. What could it be?

When the evening bell rang, she was at her place at the dining table. Her eyes met his briefly and she could feel her heart leap. She smiled at him and he returned the smile just before one man captured his attention.

She was tired but happy. Her shoulder throbbed but it didn't smother her heart rate every time she looked at him or listened to his strong, calming voice. Everything about him was highlighted now.

The men were glad to see her. Pierre brought her up to date with the condition of the ship as if she was a part of them. She listened intently, enjoying the food set before her. The entire atmosphere had transformed since the storm.

Roberto could not help but stare at her with a sheepish grin on his face. Everyone knew his feelings, since he had confessed it loudly enough. That was his own stupidity, but it was no use in fighting it. He knew from the moment he saw her in the harbour of Lisbon he had lost his heart. And it had almost cost her life for him to recognize his feelings for her. Now he was not willing to let her go and he hoped that she would trust him enough to protect her the best way possible. Once she was in the Falcon's hands there would be no way of protecting her. He had to act while still on the open seas. But to do that he needed her trust and love.

Once he was back on the upper deck, after the storm, the men had been congratulating him. There was much bantering among the men, which he took with a gracious smile, accepting it as part of his life.

Now as he watched her, he knew what he was about to offer to her was the only way to protect her and he was willing to do it.

Later she excused herself stifling a yawn behind a hand and Roberto knew this would not be the best time to talk to her about this important subject. This would change both their lives in an instant.

146

He followed, making sure she was safe in her cabin before he too returned to his own cabin to bring his journal up to date.

14

Several days later Rosa-Lee was nearly healed after the storm. The bruises on her face were almost completely gone and the shoulder was without pain although still tender to the touch. The rest of the bruises were now something of the past and the relationship between Roberto and Rosa-Lee had grown. She was now more aware of him as a man. His constant companionship convincing her that he was genuine in his feelings. His courting was obvious as he spent time with her, making sure her needs were met. What amazed her was that he did not care what the men said in passing. They joked about his affections when they were on the upper deck. The hardened pirate was all soft and mellow in her presence and she learned more about him during this time. Still he did not speak about the thing he wanted to ask her. She could see how he stopped himself on several occasions and when she asked him about this, he said he was waiting for her to heal completely which she thought was considerate of him. But still it kept her wakeful most nights, her feelings in turmoil.

One thing she knew was that she was not indifferent to him as he had put it. She cared about him. She felt safe in his presence. The man captured her thoughts as days went by and their destination came closer and closer.

She and Pierre also developed a friendship under the vigilance of Roberto. The three spoke about life at sea, the stars and many more subjects in great depth. Roberto was always taking care of her, which caused a lot of banter between the two friends. Their relationship had been born a few years back when Roberto had saved Pierre's life. One could not miss the respect and devotion between the two. They knew each other well.

One evening, just after the meal, Roberto had to attend to some paperwork in his cabin and she went out on the upper deck to stroll in the moonlight. By now, her wounds had healed. Her face still as flawless as before, and secretly she valued just a little bit more. The only scar left was on her shoulder, the only reminder of that night, a night filled with fear, but also with the revelation of Roberto's love for her.

The doctor assured her that with time it too would fade. Wearing her hair in such a manner that it covered the shoulder from public view. Twice Roberto removed the soft strands to touch the deep pink scar, his eyes smouldering with passion. That passion ignited her own heart and she felt drawn to him.

The previous evening while taking her for a stroll he once again did so and planted a soft kiss on it. His lips barely brushed her skin but left her breathless. She wondered how it would feel to be loved by him. There was no rush in his action as he stroked her neck and shoulder and told her how beautiful she looked. She was lost in his eyes and when the moment passed, she felt deprived, her body shivering at the loss.

She loved the evening walks; the sea breeze in her long hair, the sound of the ship cleaving the waters. It always made her feel that she was a part of something bigger. Sometimes he would tell her something funny that had happened during the day that made her laugh loudly.

Over the past few days she and Roberto became good friends. He never mentioned his feelings again and she left it there, searching her own heart for the feelings she had for him.

She told him about their life in Portugal as landowners, the tension among the people, and other landowners not listening to the complaints.

The villagers had caused a few funny moments, which she told with zeal. She really missed them all.

One night when Roberto was called away Rosa-Lee continued walking alone. When she came to the port side, she noticed a figure in the shadows. At first, she gave it no attention since there were always men around, and screamed when a cold, calloused hand pressed her down.

Roberto, engrossed in his work, heard the scream. Every bone in his body came to life. Immediately he rushed up to the upper deck. When his eyes were used to the darkness around him, he saw two figures struggling on the port side.

He could make out that the one had to be Rosa-Lee because of her dress. He rushed over, hearing a blunt voice speaking to her in a frightful manner. Anger filled Roberto when he realized what was going on. The man held her down tight against the railing.

"Come on, Señorita, one kiss," he hissed with a lustful tone.

"No! Leave me alone!" she screamed, struggling in his hold.

He smirked again. She tried to get away, pushing and slapping him with one hand she had managed to free but he was too strong for her.

"Stop!" Roberto shouted out. "Who is there?"

Startled, the dark figure looked at him, pushed her hard against the railing and ran away.

It looked like the new sailor; the one man that he did not trust on his ship. Roberto followed him as he ran down the steps to the lower deck right into the arms of the doctor who was on his way up. The doctor seized him. When Roberto caught up with him, he was seething.

He did not take too kindly to men that forced themselves on ladies, especially his lady.

"You were out of line, sailor." His voice was stern and cold.

"Yeah, but she is worth it. I want to have a taste of that lady as much as you do." He was arrogant and defiant.

"With one difference. The lady is not interested in you, you rat! Her scream made her intentions well-known." Roberto clipped out.

Pierre just heard the commotion and came out of his cabin, hearing the last words of the defiant.

"They all like to scream until you kiss them and then they become like putty in your hands," the sailor bragged.

"You reckon? Pierre, take him away. We will deal with him in the morning." Roberto said in a low, cold tone.

When he stalked out, the arrogant bastard called out behind him, "I will have my turn." Roberto turned around. With lightning speed and with one blow to the jaw he sent him against Pierre with a thud. The sailor was silent as blood formed on his lip.

"Bastard lock him up!" he seethed. With one pull Pierre led him away.

Roberto ran upstairs as Rosa-Lee came towards him, rubbing her arms, shaking from the sudden scare.

"Are you all right, my Rosa?" he asked the moment he saw her. He opened his arms and she stepped in as he folded her into his chest.

It was the second time that she had heard the term of endearment and her heart sped up.

"I am all right. A little shaky." She wrapped her arms around his neck without any hesitation and stood in his embrace, her head on his shoulder. For a while, they stood there, the thumping of his heart in her ears. It was a beautiful sound to her, a sound filled with love and hope.

He caressed her until he could feel that she relaxed against him and then let her go.

"Again, my hero," she said, smiling. "It's becoming a trend now."

He smiled. "I will always protect you." Drawing her closer, he placed a kiss on her forehead.

"When are you going to talk to me?" she whispered in his coat and he pushed her slightly away, searching her eyes. All he saw was trust, and *could it be? Love?* He pressed her against him and said, "Follow me," and directed her down the stairs to his cabin. Which was larger than hers.

Once inside with the door closed, he offered her wine, since she was still trembling, and sat next to her.

Each took a few sips to calm them from the sudden rush. He looked at her, making sure she was all right, and placed his glass on the desk.

Rosa-Lee watched in awe as Roberto knelt before her, removing the glass from her hand, and asked,

"How do you feel about me?" his dark ochre eyes were wide and serious. Careful curiosity filled them as he watched her. His face was still stern, but a muscle rippled in his jaw. He was nervous, she realized, and whatever he wanted to ask was causing this.

Her answer was critical to him. He held both her hands in a firm grip, his tension real.

For several days she had thought about her feelings and the things he invoked in her. His presence was secure and strong. He was not afraid of admitting how he felt. She knew she cared for him, trusted him, but could it be love? Last night as she had read her parents' journals once again, she realized the love she had seen and the emotions she felt for him were the same. She could not deny it anymore.

"I love you, Roberto," she whispered, and light dawned in the ochre eyes so that they were more of a rich golden colour. Surprise and joy filled his face. The scar she had come to love softened and creases formed over his cheeks. "Really?"

"Yes, I am sure." He lowered his head and brushed against her lips. "Marry me." She gasped with delight and shock. Her body trembled, and she stared wide-eyed up to him. Did she hear right? *Marriage. Did he just propose?*

"Marry me, my Rosa," he repeated, this time louder. She could not help but just stare as his lips touched her once again. He was hesitant and soft at first before he took her mouth hungrily. She leaned into him and returned the kiss. She was warm and inviting and when he finally pulled back, she smiled. "You know how to pursue a girl," and giggled.

"Does that mean it is a yes?" he asked with a smile breaking over his whole face.

She nodded. "Yes."

"Rosa, my Rosa." and she vanished into his embrace as he devoured her lips once again.

It was a while before they broke apart and he sat down and held her hand, visibly trembling with excitement.

Roberto could not believe that this brave and stunning woman had agreed to be his wife. She was everything he wanted.

It was late when he returned her to her cabin, light-headed with the love he felt for her. When he entered his cabin, Pierre arrived and informed him the pirate who had attacked Rosa-Lee was ranting in his cell and not happy at all.

Roberto dismissed the subject and Pierre looked at the Captain in stunned disbelief. He knew Roberto was smitten with Rosa-Lee, but it was worse. He never thought he would see the pirate fall for a woman like Captain Roberto did for Rosa-Lee. It pleased him greatly.

†††

The next morning at six, the sailor was flogged. When Rosa-Lee heard the first lash, she hurried onto the upper deck, stepping closer till she was just behind Roberto. The crew were looking at their crewmate with disgust. The news had spread amongst them.

The man received ten lashes and was untied. When he fell on the deck, salt water was poured over him. He flinched without making a sound. When he spotted her behind Roberto he smirked, his beady eyes sending a clear message. *I will be back.* She shivered.

"Take him below," Pierre instructed with a stern voice. Roberto turned and saw her standing there. He smiled, his love visible in the depths of his eyes.

"Good morning *Môn Petite* are you feeling better?"

"Yes, Captain, thanks once again," she said respectfully, lifting her lips to receive a soft kiss.

"Let's go and eat. I am starving." She looped her arm into his with a smile playing over her face.

After breakfast he took her to his cabin and said, "I want us to get married today." She gasped. She had hardly slept last night. The pure thrill of being in his arms, of loving him was so new that it kept her up. She looked at him in surprise and wonder, "But why so quickly?"

"Why not?" came the gruff reply. "I love you and don't want to wait. Last night just confirmed how vulnerable you are on this ship."

"But you saved me. There is no need to be in a hurry. Besides, I would love to have my parents present."

"No," he said, unexpectedly loud.

"No?"

"No, Rosa-Lee. I asked, you to trust me and this is the only way I know how to ensure your safety."

"But Roberto, I can defend myself," she insisted.

"Not against men like the Falcon and that pirate last night. You are too precious to me. Besides," and he wrapped her in his arms, "I want to love you." He kissed her until she was breathless, and she chuckled as she gave herself to him, her arms around his neck. All shyness was gone as she gave herself over to the bliss he offered. She understood what he meant. She had never been with a man before and he did things to her that were unknown to her but exciting. She had to admit she wanted more than just this.

But still, this was too soon. And what would her parents say of this sudden marriage? Her marriage to a *pirate* no less. As much as she cared for him, would her love persuade her parents to allow this wedding to take place? Her father was always clear in his feelings towards pirates and for her to bring him home would ensure heartache. She did not want to be the one who caused them any more grief. Questions poured through her, bringing her back to reality.

Her smile faltered briefly, and she dropped her arms to her sides. She tried to move away but he did not let her.

Roberto saw the change, stopped her, and lifted her chin with a finger. His eyes were wary as he looked upon her youthful face.

"What is wrong, Rosa?"

Her eyes were wide with concern and hesitance. "Roberto." She did not want to let him know about her concerns and she pushed him away, her breath swallow as she tried to gather her wits. But this was important to her. "I really want my parents to witness this occasion. You know how I feel about them." *Among others,* she thought, not meeting his gaze. But he was a very perceptive man and forced her back to him.

"That is not your biggest concern though?" She swallowed. She could not lie to him or be dishonest.

"Rosa-Lee, look at me," he insisted. "It is because of what I am, isn't it?" She looked at him in dismay. "Roberto ..." But he put a finger on her lips, quieting her. "Rosa, I know my occupation is not desirable for any woman, or her family, but if you trust me everything will work out at the end."

"How, Roberto?"

"You will see, my love," He kissed her softly.

"Roberto," she whispered and clasped his arms. He looked at her, his own thoughts buried deep in his mind where she would not be able to see. For now, he had to convince her that this marriage was important not only to him but to her safety.

"I know, my love, but once I have returned you safely back to Portugal, we can talk to your father and have the great occasion you want. But for now, my men will be the only guests at our wedding." His authoritative voice left no room for argument. She looked at him with concern etched in her mind. She knew her father would understand once he was past the initial shock, but still, it could put a damper on their happiness. She really loved the man that stood in front of her. Her whole being cried out to be with him. She touched his face once again. Worry and concern stood out in the lines of his mouth and eyes and she want to remove that. She wanted to be part of him. Another question dawned on her and she started to chuckle, her eyes filled with merriment as she asked.

"Who would marry us?"

"Pierre is also a captain," he said as a smile softened his own features and he pulled her closer. "Does this mean yes?"

She smiled. "Not to sound like a parrot but you do know how to change my mind." He chuckled as his mouth once again captured her mouth.

Minutes later he released her and said softly, "You make me a happy man."

"Yes?"

"Yes." And he kissed her. "Let me go to Pierre and tell him the wedding is on."

"You already talked to him?"

"Yes."

"You are conceited, Mr Pirate."

"I cannot help it, it is my nature, and you do this to me, my Rosa." She groaned softly when he kissed her again.

15

That afternoon, when the announcement came that they were getting married, roars of laughter and cheers of exuberance resonated all over the deck.

Pierre did the honours and married them. A feast was prepared under the blue heavens for all to enjoy. The celebration continued for the rest of the day and night.

Roberto was smiling non-stop, holding her close to him, never once letting her go. She wrapped around him like gift-wrap. She looked amazing in a white taffeta dress with silver threads embroidered on the bodice, enhancing every curve to Roberto's delight. Her hair waved behind her beneath a tiara he had given her that morning. Rubies in the form of a rose were imbedded in the tiara. She looked ravishing. His gaze was on her, covering her with his love.

Later in his cabin they melted together, and she allowed him to love her as he promised. All shyness disappeared as he explored every inch of her. He took his time in teaching her about her own desires and what inflamed him the most. They only came up for air to eat and bathe in the morning, then returned to explore once again the wonder of the new-found love.

She realized that she had so much to learn about him but at that moment what they shared was more than enough.

Ten days later another storm hit the *Contra O Vento*. Everyone scurried around to tie everything down to the ship. The winds were strong and icy cold against their skins. Dark menacing clouds formed around them, and waves came crushing down, leaving them all drenched.

Rosa-Lee was helping when she felt strong arms grabbing her from behind. A big hand covered her mouth. Kicking, she was picked up as if she was a feather and carried downstairs to her old cabin. She kicked against the walls to stop him, but he simply forced her legs under his arm. She could not fight the strength of the hands holding her tightly. Her door was slammed open and she was unceremoniously thrown on her old bed, drenched to the bone. When she finally could see who it was she steeled herself against the brute. She looked into the rat's small eyes, dripping wet with lust, fixed on her. She scrambled away but he grabbed her leg, bringing her closer to the edge.

"Finally, we are alone, Señorita. They are all so busy that they will not notice you are gone, and I am going to take my time with you," he snarled. She knew it was futile to scream, no one would hear her. She would have to defend herself.

He grabbed the skirt and she could hear the material rip. One shoe fell with a thud on the floor. The other she had lost during the struggle.

"Your captain cannot save you. You are mine," he seethed. "Did you really think that those lashes would stop me? I want you!"

"NO!" she screamed, desperate to get away and fought harder against him. Nevertheless, he pulled her closer, pressing his full weight on her as he spoke.

"I promise I will have you." He planted a wet kiss on her lips, and she bit him. Lust changed into hate and he slapped her while swearing. Straightening himself, he tore at her clothing, determined to get to her.
Her bodice laces were hanging loose in front of her chest. He lowered his head to her breast, closing hungry lips around her.

Forcefully, she pushed him away. One side of her dress tore under his grip, revealing more skin, and he laughed, pinning her down with a leg as he shed his shirt, revealing a bulky, hairy chest.

She willed herself to be calm and to think. Screaming would not help. They would not hear her through the wailing winds, the creaking ship and crushing waters. She had to act to protect herself and with shaking fingers, she kicked and reached for the pillows in a moment he let go of her. She knew her weapons were still there. She had left them when they got married along with everything else. This was the first time she had been back in her old cabin.

To protect herself, Rosa-Lee had placed her dagger underneath her pillow after the last attack. Now she had to get to it, stretching her body as far as possible. This could not happen to her, not after she experienced love and pleasure at the hand of her husband.

He grabbed her feet, forcing himself in between her legs with an ugly, lustful grin. She kicked again to move herself up closer to the pillows. She stretched again as he tore her petticoat, her legs exposed before him. He released a guffaw that vibrated through her fear. His rough hands stroking her thighs as he tore more fabric away.

With a final effort she reached the dagger, grabbing it tightly while looking intently at the man who was so engrossed with her, muttering incoherent words she did not understand, and lifted the blade to his face.

Lust dazed he did not notice the knife in her hand, his eyes fixed on her inner thighs, spreading her. With an ugly laugh still on his lips she plunged the blade into his neck with a forceful grunt. Disbelief changed his entire face. Blood were spewing from his neck unto her, and she pushed him further away. The knife hanging lose and then fell unto her.

With all her strength she pushed and kicked at the limp body. The man was heavy, and she struggled some more until she could get rid of him and he finally fell on the wooden floor. Wide eyes stared up to her and with some effort she scrambled over him to get away.

Meanwhile Pierre came down with valuable cargo and was stopped abruptly. He froze at the picture in front of him, a bloody Rosa-Lee stood just inside the doorframe, completely still. The metallic stench of blood floated in the cabin.

Stepping closer he saw the rat on the floor. A gaping wound in his neck told its own story. He was dead before he knew it.

Trembling, she covered herself. Pierre took a blanket and wrapped her in it. For a moment he just stood there, holding her shaking body until she let go.

"Thanks Pierre."

"I will get Roberto, can you stand?" she nodded and leaned against the frame just outside the cabin. The sight of the man nauseating.

Commotion broke lose as Roberto ran down the passage, minutes later. At first glance he saw the man on the floor and then reached for Rosa-Lee. Staring at him she said softly, "It is the first time I killed a man," through clenched teeth. Tears started to run down her cheeks.

"Did he hurt you?"

"A few scratches, but I am fine." She assured him.

The doctor entered the cabin, knelt at the body and confirmed the death of the sailor. With a sheet he covered the face and closed the door behind him as Roberto took her away. He would be dealt with later.

At their cabin the doctor examined her under the close eyes of her husband and gave her something for the shock and pain. Still shivering she was in a dreadful state. Her dress torn she felt uncomfortable the entire time. Not letting go of the blanket. The doctor respected that and once he ensured the captain that she was still intact, he left. Immediately she clung to Roberto. Her body's trembling a giveaway of whet she felt. The bruises that had formed from the manhandling disguised under her tattered dress.

She could hear his heart racing, echoing her own. He then lifted her, sat down and placed her on his lap, covering her face with warm kisses.

"Before you sleep, we must get you out of this wet clothing, my love."

She nodded softly, numbness in her limbs. She was so cold that she shivered uncontrollably, all the past few weeks" ordeals coming down in one swift move, the cold, the storms, the absence of her parents, the attack, and the death. The tears were unstoppable.

Roberto could only hold her next to his drenched body while he caressed her. His heart throbbed for her. He made her stand up,

164

which she reluctantly aloud. Once he removed the blanket he yelped in shock. She was covered with blood. Her dress torn, with a final rush of anger he stripped the wet dress from her. Hatred in his eyes told its own story before he looked at his wife again.

She stood there shivering. Wide spread eyes watching him carefully. He gave her a rueful smile and whispered softly how sorry he was for not being there, laying kisses over her breasts. She allowed him the time even though everything screamed to cover herself. She felt violated but realized it was important for them both to reconnect.

A few moments later he rubbed her dry with a towel, drying her long hair where it fell over her breasts, concealing them from him. Finally, he placed her underneath the covers.

Eyes closed, she looked pale and tired as he watched her while stripping himself. He lay down next to her, covering himself, nestling her closer to him. They both fell asleep, once he was certain she was all right.

It was almost dusk when Rosa-Lee stirred in his arms. By now he was already awake, watching her sweet face next to him, propped up on one arm. Thinking of the naked body in his bed made his own to act in arousal, but that had to wait.

When she opened her eyes, she looked bewildered. The memories of the previous night came back in a flash. For a moment she did not know where she was.

"You are safe." He whispered, and she pulled him closer, holding him tightly. When he put his arms around her, the sheets moved down, revealing a soft shoulder and the slope of her breast. He leaned down and removed her hair, the scar still visible, but he didn't mind kissing it softly. He could feel her tremble under his touch, relaxing into him.

He moved her up toward him pressed against his hard chest. He held on tightly and enjoyed her soft body against him, his hands brushing the soft skin.

Seeing the place where the man left a bruise on her soft skin, he touched it. Rosa-Lee watched as he traced the long bruise over her nipple, raw emotions playing over his face echoing her own feelings. His gentle touch was so different from the brute of last night and she moaned with delight.

"I am so sorry for not being there," he finally said in a whisper. Just thinking of what could have happened replayed another time, a time he would much rather forget. He had almost lost her like he had lost his sister, and tears rolled down his cheeks.

Rosa-Lee felt the wetness on her skin and lifted his face. "This is not your fault my love. I do not blame you."

"I vowed to protect you," he said. "So far I am not doing a very fine job of it."

"You are everything I want in a man. Please, love, don't punish yourself about this," she whispered and kissed him, wiping away the wetness. I am here and safe. That is all that matters"

"If any harm should come to you, I would never forgive myself," he said softly.

"Nothing can happen to me. Beside I am married to a mean pirate." She smiled at him and he chuckled.

"I do not feel like that right now."

"What, my brave and fearless pirate is terrified?" Trying to make light of this Rosa-Lee could see the effect of the ordeal on him. "Nothing has changed, love. You are still the only man for me. I trust you."

He looked at her as if she was saying something profound. "Really?"

"Yes, my love, really. Now go and get me some clothes."

"Yes, ma'am." He kissed her before he jumped out of bed. Rosa-Lee fell back on the soft mattress where she still could feel his warmth. Taking deep breaths, she would not show him how much last night shook her. It was over. She was safe. That was all that mattered.

"I will get Enrico to get you a dress." She nodded as she watched him putting on his now familiar black breeches and white shirt followed by long black boots and black belt.

He pulled a cord, and, in a few seconds, Enrico was at the door.

"Enrico, please bring the señorita's night gown and then prepare some food for her."

"Yes, Captain."

Rosa-Lee protested. "I want a dress, Roberto."

"No, you will stay in bed and that is an order, Rosa-Lee." His tone was stern and authoritative.

167

"Yes, Captain." She smiled. It was no use to argue with him once he made up his mind.

Enrico was back in minutes with her nightgown. Roberto helped her to dress and Enrico asked. "Should I bring your food here as well, Captain?"

"Yes." the moment Enrico stepped out Roberto placed a kiss on her cheek, and she smiled.

With the brush she started to brush her hair, all tangled with sea salt.

"Let me." He took the brush from her and continued. At first, he had to remove many tangles but eventually her hair was straight and shining. The simple act was reassuring as the silk fell through his fingers.

"Thanks, Roberto," she whispered, feeling loved and cosy with the affection. She never thought that a man could be so gentle like this man. Since they got married, he cared for her. Nothing was amiss, and she felt truly loved and adored. There were times that her thoughts wanted to overshadow the happiness but then she would push them away. She made the choice to marry him and what she got was a loving and caring husband. The mean man she met months ago was gone. Even his crew treated her with respect.

She looked around his now-familiar cabin. *A man's holy place,* her father had once said. *If you want to know the man you must look at his room that will tell you much about him.* His scent was all over the cabin, a distinct smell that mixed with sea, wind, cigars and earth. Not even her own fragrance could extinguish his smell. And she loved it would not change it for anything.

Books filled a bookshelf near the window and on an end table. A book lay open next to an easy chair, worn out at the armrests.

That was his place of solitude. Many times, he would sit there and pull her in his lap, and they would listen to the crashing of the waves against the hull of the ship or the wind's wailing when the sea was boisterous and playful. Those were the times she cherished the most because then he opened himself to her and she would learn more about the man. The pirate was in the back, lingering.

Dark colours covered the bed and windows. In the one corner was a glass cabinet filled with weapons and swords.

The desk was well-organized. No papers lay around. In fact, everything was organized neatly, and yet it had a sense of homeliness.

Roberto watched her as she studied his cabin and then asked, "Do you like what you see?"

"Yes, it is you. I don't want to change anything. Your love for books astounds me."

He chuckled. "Why? Do you think all pirates are ignorant?" he asked as he walked toward her.

"No." She chuckled with a blush. "You are quite surprising for a pirate."

"I am glad to have the lady's approval." He kissed her soundly.

169

"You are everything I want in a man," she added. He chuckled.

"I am glad to hear that." He kissed her again and rose once again "You can read some if you like."

"I would like that," and closed her eyes for a second.

"What happened to the man?" She could not believe what she had done. She tried to forget the events of the previous night, but it came back, and she had to know.

"He met a watery grave."

"I've caused a lot of problems for you?"

"No, sooner or later he would have betrayed me, I never liked him. You did me a favour." He walked to his desk to collect some water for her.

"I was so afraid."

"I know, but you are safe now. The rest of the crew adores you. They were furious when they heard what the man tried to do. If you had not killed him one of them would have." He handed her the glass which she gratefully took, drinking the cool water with one gulp. When the glass was empty, she gave it back to him. He returned to the table.

"What happened to your sister?" This was the one question she wanted to ask but avoided so far. He stilled at the table and answered softly, "She hung herself after the rape." Sorrow filled his face. It was still hard after all these years.

Softly she got to her feet and walked over to him standing near the window. This time she comforted him, wrapping her arms around his waist.

"How old was she?"

"Twenty- one." The stoic reply sent shivers up her spine.

"She had just learned that she was pregnant with the man's baby, and then she hung herself."

"I am so sorry for your loss."

"It's all right. It was a very long time ago."

After a few minutes of silence, looking out into the bright sky, she turned her gaze back to him and said,

"I am so confused about you. It would be so easy to love you, but your lifestyle, your choices. I do not understand. You do not act like a pirate, yet you are one. My father always said we must never judge a book by its cover. When I open yours it gives me joy, but it is difficult to look past the cover." her eyes filled with sincere emotions of expectation. "Why did you choose this lifestyle?"

He could see genuineness in her posture when she asked the question. She is trying very hard to make sense out of this. He wrapped her in his arms, thankful for her understanding and acceptance. It could not be easy. He owed her some answers.

"I did not choose it. It chose me," he finally answered.

"Don't you want to tell me?" suddenly they were interrupted with a hard knock and she quickly went to the door, took the food from Enrico and closed the door. Hastily she took it over to the table where they sat and proceeded to fill their plates.

The entire time he waited for her to sat down again. Time he thought of his life and knew he owed her the truth.

"Please, Roberto, tell me so that I can understand," she said again, encouraging him after handing him his plate.

"I am a farmer by birth." He smiled when he saw disbelief written on her face and continued.

"My parents have a huge farm on the south coast of France. We were happy in those days. We loved one another and the joy of working in the fields made me content. I loved the land, the smell of breaking ground, the whole process of planting and waiting, and then the harvest." He smiled, his thoughts far away.

"Then, four years in a row we had very bad drought and no harvests. My father fell into debt and finally it was time to pay up. The lender who helped my father was the cousin of the Falcon. My sister and I were given as slaves to pay off the debt. It was the hardest thing my parents had to do but we understood."

She gasped, placing a hand on his arm. "How old were you?" The food was forgotten on their plates.

"I was nineteen, my sister twenty-one."

16

"Veronica was raped on the first night, while we were still on the ship taking us to the Falcon's lair. Two months later she became sick with morning sickness. One slave girl said she was pregnant. The absolute devastation caused her to hang herself. Everyone knew what had happened to her and everyone made the connection.

When I heard about it two days later, I was bitter and full of rage, seeking the man that had done this to her. I killed him later. Hence the scar." Roberto smirked, and Rosa-Lee squeezed his arm. Raw emotions shadowed his face as she watched Roberto reliving those dreadful times. How tragic to not only lose the home you knew for nineteen years but a beloved sister in such a barbaric way.

Rosa-Lee reached out to him and grabbed his hand, holding him to her heart. She uttered no words as she listened to his life story.

"The Falcon was so impressed with me that he took me under his wing and taught me everything I know about sailing and piracy. He is a very clever man and I learned a lot. I was eager to learn everything, and at the age of twenty-five he adopted me as his son." He looked at her pleadingly, hoping that she would still love him. She laid a hand on his cheek, the action solemn and caring. Her eyes were set unwaveringly on him and he smiled as his face relaxed in the knowledge that she did not despise him. He kissed her palm reverently.

She smiled and asked, "How did you meet Pedro?"

"He was on your father's ship when we captured it. The cargo was of much importance to the Falcon. After a long battle and many lives lost it was in our hands. I first noticed Pedro as he killed two of our men. He was apprehended immediately. He gave a good fight, I might add," sighed softly and continued.

"When Falcon heard whose son he was, he was impressed. Your father is well-known. His bravery and leadership are respected by all on the seven seas, both sailors and pirates. I have told you that the crew adores you because you are his daughter. They respected him although they never met him." he smiled at her and she returned the smile.

"At night Pedro had to tell us about the adventures on the sea and in Africa. He mentioned you many times. I was intrigued with you and when the Falcon came up with the plan to ask for a ransom, I volunteered. Your brother's stories didn't do you justice. You are more impressive in real life."

Silence fell between them as they locked gazes again, seeing each other, the hardship that had moulded them to become the people they were. Understanding dawned on Rosa-Lee's heart and she smiled, a smile which reached the dark brown eyes. Roberto pulled her closer and kissed her, demanding. She came closer, opening herself to him.

"I am sorry for the position you are in but not sorry that I have met you." Roberto said softly as he brushed her hair from her eyes, and she kissed him on the cheek.

"I know what you mean," She replied. "We would have never met if it was not for the ransom."

"No, although I am sure I would have found another way. You have captured my mind and my heart swiftly. My body had no other choice but to follow."

She chuckled. "For a pirate you are very romantic." Their lips brushed lightly.

"Please don't tell anyone," he murmured.

"No. It is my secret tucked in my heart. I love you, Roberto de Ville."

"I love you, Rosa-Lee de Ville." He swept her from her feet and onto the bed in record time.

Later they let go of each other and ate from the food on the table. He stood up to light more lanterns and sat down again next to her.

"You had an interesting life, Roberto, and it is true what my father said, you cannot judge a book by its cover." Her smile was shy, but her eyes looked at him like he hoped she would.

The last few weeks had been filled with discovery for him. His recklessness to expose his heart was a revelation. Usually he kept everything for himself but with her, he just blurted it out. He wanted her to know him, to love him and was not ashamed to answer uncomfortable questions. In the process she opened as well. He could still feel her soft skin under his hand, the soft roundness of her curves as she burned with passion. His body was in permanent desire for her, to know her intimately. She opened to him unabashedly, pliant under his coaching.

"One day you must tell me about your parents and the farm. I would love to hear more."

"I will do so, but I think we need to go and sleep. You are still very tired," Roberto said, standing up. "Let me put you in bed." He held his arm out and she slipped her arm into his.

As they walked to bed, they were both overcome with the emotions from the previous night, the new discoveries and melted into each other. There was nothing that could compare to this bonding.

When he turned to her finally, out of breath, his eyes were again that dark ochre colour. He wrapped her in his arms and whispered,

"I love you. Since the moment I saw you, my Rosa, I've loved you. I want you to know that and I will never get tired of saying it." She placed a hand on his chest and kissed him on the lips. He pulled her closer and demanded her to open her mouth once again, passion flowing as they kissed. His mouth was pleading and demanding to let him in, to love her, his hands burning her skin, setting her heart racing, like butterflies fluttering and the momentum of their wings driving her closer to him. It was as if they could not get enough. All was forgotten except to just live for the moment.

She moved even closer to him, as desire coursed through her body, a serene feeling that made her breathless. She could feel his body reacting to her.

"I want you so much," The things that this man did to her were wonderful, intoxicating and she gave him his heart's desire.

"My Rosa." His body was trembling with the need to have her, his lips craving her body, and she responded.

†††

Every day they passed each other on the deck. The magnitude of their hearts; the passion of their bodies drew them closer. At times when it became too unbearable, he would open his arms and she would step in, seeking his closeness, listening to his steady heartbeat.

They would talk, and he would open more to her the things that were important. Her resistance crumbled under the care and love she received.

Pierre would tell of his bravery on many occasions. The bond of friendship between the two men was tight, since they shared many journeys together.

On occasion Pierre would meet up with her when Roberto was engaged with work and although he was quieter, they had a lot in common. Pierre would tell her about their journeys in detail depicting Roberto as a good leader although a pirate. They were not ashamed of their vocation and sometimes she would tremble with fear and then laugh in joy. She always felt safe though, with Pierre and the rest of the crew.

At times, when alone her mind would drift to her parents left behind in Portugal. What would be their reaction to her sudden marriage to the man that abducted her from her home? She thought about her brother Manuel and the man he had become; about Pedro and the path he had chosen for himself. And of course, she thought about Roberto, her husband, and what life held for them.

Would they have a future?

Here on the open seas he was safe but once on land he would have to stay hidden. He would always be on the run from the authorities, living in the shadows, and where would that put her? How would she go on knowing that any day he could be arrested and hanged? Because there would be no mercy once he was caught. Could she really live a life on the run, with uncertainty her only constant? What if children were born out of this union? Where would it put them?

She had so many questions always in the back of her mind and when she watched him, she was terrified of the life she agreed to live with him. He said she was brave, but she was not. The mere thought of him being killed left her shaken with fear.

Roberto himself had problems of his own. He would watch her as she strolled down the deck, deep in thought. He knew that he had done the right thing to marry her. She made him happy and he felt content with her being his wife. But if everything worked out as he hoped could he continue being happy with her? Would she not regret this marriage? It was so much for her to trust him without knowing the truth. She trusted him.

Fear gripped him many times and on occasions like that Pierre would sweep in and change his thoughts. He was the only one he could trust with his feelings and his future. He was the only one that knew what this could cost him if he failed.

I cannot fail. I cannot lose her.

Never!

†††

A month later, another storm hit them. The day quickly turned into night as thunderous black clouds formed in the sky.

The swells of the seas grew bigger and higher with every passing minute. It looked terrifying. The waves stood ten feet high, towering over them before they crashed down on top of them. One mast broke because of the weight, and the ship was tossed and rolled with every breaking wave.

High-speed winds went through them, leaving them cold and helpless. A few of the men were tossed overboard and Roberto instructed Rosa-Lee to stay down in the lower decks where she helped, carrying water and comforting the hurting men.

It went on for three days. The ship creaked dangerously but kept together. Everyone tensed every time another deafening crack vibrated through the woodwork, holding their breaths until the ship rolled again. Exhausted, the men fell asleep and slept in shifts during this time. The cook prepared a warm stew that the men gobbled up. Their arms felt heavy. Every muscle felt torn from the inside. The doctor worked right through to aid the men in their discomfort, salving blisters and torn muscles, removing splinters, stitching up head wounds, bandaging broken bones. They were in pitiful shape.

In all this time Rosa-Lee hardly saw Roberto, only hearing his barking voice as he gave orders, demanded action, motivated the men. His voice was scarcely audible over the high wind and tossing waves. He hardly took a break, irritated when she came close to offer him food or water, sending her right back below.

Finally, when it became quieter, Roberto stumbled into their cabin, soaked, exhausted. When she looked for him later she found him sprawled on the bed, too tired to bother with the wet clothes. He was snoring lightly, his head pushed in the pillows, his black hair plastered against his face. Softly she walked to him, just studying the broad back, ripped shirt, the narrow waist with the incredible long legs.

She knew she loved him. As she watched him, she knew he was the one for her, the one she had waited for all her life. She had no doubt in her mind any more. His love warmed her up and she gave to him what he wanted, her love.

At first, she hesitated, but she knew she could not leave him in this state. She wanted to take care of him as he had cared for her many times. She wanted him to know that she cared more. With trembling hands, she started to push him to the side. She had to get to the buttons to strip the wet clothes from his body.

The moment she touched him he was awake. Her small hands were trying to roll him, pressing against his body. He rolled on his back and watched her out of hazy eyes, enjoying her touch on his skin. He watched the emotions on her face, the tenderness as she looked at him, her hands brushing over the length of him. A soft, womanly smile played over her lips, dimples appearing. She was lovely.

She struggled to remove his wet boots. They clung to his feet and it took her awhile to dispose of them. He smiled at the determination with which she did the task. When she started with his breeches, he willed himself not to respond as she brushed against him. Unaware of what she did to him as she stripped the wet clothes from him. He closed his eyes and relaxed under her stare, allowing her to study him. He could feel her eyes raking over him, sure that there must be a blush on her face.

Hard and beautiful he lay in front of her, his muscles still tensed after the strenuous work. A soft mat of black hair was on his chest trailing down to his manhood. She allowed herself the freedom to let her eyes linger there and swallowed as her own body reacted, moisture pooling between her legs. He was stunning. She took in every muscle on the toned body until she ended at his face with the three-day-old stubble.

She reached for a towel, dried him, and then placed the covers over him. When she started to leave, he spoke sleepily. It startled her, and she blushed, keeping her face down. Just the mere thought of him lying there buck-naked under the covers, the fact that she had just seen him so, even though they were married, still caused the blood to sing through her veins.

"Please. Stay with me," he murmured, and then appeared to doze off. She went back to his bed and the moment she sat next to him, he turned on his side and his arms encircled her, pulling her closer, and then he was gone into sleep.

She watched him sleeping and enjoyed the feel of his skin under her fingers, tracing the muscles on the broad shoulder, following the arm. He rolled again, exposing his chest for her, her hand touching the dark nipples with curiosity as they hardened. She suppressed a giggle. He really was a handsome one.

When she had removed his shirt, she saw a few scars on his back and on his stomach, evidence of the life he led. She traced them, giving each one attention with her fingers, brushing against him. He looked like the paintings they had on the walls in the study at home; a portrait of masculinity and beauty.

It made her skin tingle with pleasure. She could feel him move closer. He turned once again, his head in her lap and his bare back exposed for her to touch.

She caressed him softly, tracing the shoulder blades with her hand, his skin soft but muscles hard, his breathing rhythmic against her.

She was also tired after the storm and somewhere during the night she dozed off, her head on her chest, her long hair touching his back.

She awoke when a hand cupped a breast and when she opens her eyes, he was very close to her, his head lifted, lying on her bosom. He tangled his hand into her hair, bringing her head down, and then kissed her with a burning passion. He lifted himself more against her and her arms went around him, drawing him closer, opening her mouth. The exploring of their tongues ignited fire in them both. She could feel his hands busy with the lace of the bodice.

"I need you, my Rosa," he whispered against her lips.

"Yes. Me too. It was too long." She arched toward him, his hand rough but soft on her bare skin.

"How much...?" he encouraged.

"I love you!" she finally could say, out of breath.

"Tell me again, how much?" His voice strained with bottled up emotions, his hands untying the laces of her skirt, pressing the

182

material down. With a thump they fell on the floor. He removed her petticoat, pressing kisses on her flat stomach.

"I love you," she managed to say again; butterflies scattering around her stomach and throat. With a groan he lifted himself, drawing her underneath him until they were back on the bed, pressing her into the softness, and he kissed her all over.

Her skin electrified under his touch. The sensations of desire flooded her very being and she was ready for him. Her body trembled under every touch as his fingers moved into the core of her excitement.

Moans left her mouth that he smothered with his own as she gasped. He took her to a high plain of heated desire. She wrapped her legs around his hips, clamping him, and then with a thrust he was in her, taking her, claiming her as his own.

Her brain exploded with him inside of her. She felt dizzy and said, "I love you," which brought him to a fruitful climax.

To experience the wonder of his love after the storm was too much and tears ran down her face. Her eyes shone with adoration as she brought him closer and kissed him.

Roberto was in a blissful state of his own. He had never had this kind of passion, never felt as intimate with a woman as with his Rosa, kissing her with heated kisses, hungry for her touch.

He held her, imbedded in her. She did not let go. She whispered in his ear, "More, my love," and he complied, whispering, "I love you, my Rosa." He turned her around as she whimpered from the release. He smiled, stroking her lower back to relax her, lifting her hips, exposing her. He took her again. She gasped for breath.

Moans vibrated through her again as she reached for the wall to steady herself to receive him. Again, their rhythm synchronized as they came to an orgasmic scream, breathless with desire.

He held her tight; laid his head on her back, running his hands over her, and let them rest on her with delight.

Touching her, he could not remember the last time he had experienced multiple orgasms in one.

Panting for breath, they dropped down on the mattress, he still holding her into his body, spooning into her as she lay on her side out of breath, her eyes closed.

Feeling her own heartbeat racing, she felt satiated, her body trembling under his embrace. The mattress shifted under his weight. He came up onto his knees as he turned her over again, facing her, while he cuddled her in his strong arms.

"My wife, my Rosa, I love you."

"I love you, my love," she whispered, and they dozed off into a wonderful carefree sleep.

17

Time moved on but stood still. They continued with their discoveries. The ship moved, bringing them ever closer to their destination, but for now they were blissfully unaware of this. Their nights were filled with exotic adventure.

Rosa-Lee loved the flaming path his passion had traced all through her body and showed him exactly how much, giving in to everything he did, allowing him to take her to new heights. His lips searched and kissed every part of her. She found she had spots that responded more to him. At those spots; he would linger longer, taking his time, until she pleaded with him.

He did not disappoint, teaching her the things he loved to do to her. In return, she could enjoy every part of him, lingering at the places she came to recognize as his most sensitive spots. She chuckled when he too, pleaded gruffly, her eyes shimmering with excitement.

It made her feel wanted and alive. On these occasions he would whisper, "I have created a monster," in her ear, and she chuckled with pleasure as he took her again.

He would whisper about his life and future with her, sharing his heart, and she would do the same. There was no end and no beginning. Everything began and ended with each other.

Out of breath, a sheen of perspiration covering both their bodies, he huskily said, "You are extremely passionate, my rose."

"Do you enjoy it?" she asked with desire in her voice.

"Yes, I do. I love you Rosa-Lee de Ville. You have made me the happiest man. I always had a longing to leave this pirate's world behind but never had the reason, until I met you. You are my reason to go back to be a farmer, if you will have it?" he whispered during one of these nights. He wanted to tell her so much but could not. But he did want to assure her of a future with him.

"Yes, Roberto, those are beautiful words. But how, my love?" she replied, out of breath and speechless. She never expected it. He, leaving this world behind. Her prayers were answered, and she wrapped herself around him and kissed him with joy bubbling over. He chuckled as kisses rained on him. He knew that it fettered her mind continuously.

"It is possible. Piracy was good to me, but the farm is waiting. I want to farm and make it a success, for our children one day." Kissing her, his voice turned serious.

"But, my Rose, you will have to trust me from now on to get us both out of the piracy life. You will have to be strong, stronger than before. Our safety can only be guaranteed with you trusting me."

She lifted herself up, seeing the gravity of his words and said, "There are still things that I don't understand but I will trust you unconditionally. You are my husband. Your word means everything to me."

"Where did I get you?" he sighed in contentment and he pulled her closer.

"You kidnapped me out of my parent's house, remember, Mr Pirate-man?" she chuckled.

He groaned and crushed her mouth with his again.

His Rosa.

†††

After weeks of marital bliss, the crow master called out, "Land ahoy!"

As they watched the land mass growing in front of them, Roberto became tense, silent. His voice sounded strange when he spoke.

"It is the southern point of Madagascar. We still have three days left and then we will be at the Isle of Saint Marie at the house of the Falcon. There are things that I still need to tell you, my Rosa," he said, hesitance in his voice.

"Yes, my love?" she lifted her trusting gaze to him. He swallowed hard, touching her face

"Things will be different there. Things will seem strange, and sometimes what seems true is not. There are no laws and no morals. The only law that counts is the Falcon's. He is a hard and cruel man and does not take deception lightly. The best course is always to be straightforward. Say only what is necessary." He gulped, taking in deep breaths as if he braced himself against whatever lay out there.

"I cannot stress it enough. You need to trust me and know that I love you, no matter what." Urgency filled his voice and he held her with a rigid firmness.

"Roberto, you frighten me when you talk like that! But I also believe that you have your reasons, and because I love you, I trust you. There is no doubt in my mind."

Again, the familiar, confused thoughts from the beginning entered her mind. *What is he not telling me?* She thought.

For weeks, she had seen a side of him that she adored and loved. Her feelings for him had grown. She respected him not only as her husband but also as a man. His character was not that of a pirate. Stories her father told her of them convinced her that he was not one. She did not know what to expect once they were on land. But he desperately wanted her to trust him, and that she was willing to do.

"I will never hurt you intentionally, but you need to be brave, and Rosa-Lee," he hesitated. "Trust no one else."

"Yes Roberto of course." She hugged him, anxious because of his seriousness, and he drew her closer in his embrace.

"Roberto, what are you not telling me?" she asked after a while, her heart beating loud in her chest. Panic filled her.

"Always remember that I love you. All will be revealed at the end. That is all I can say for now. Keep on trusting me," He said in a desperate plea, crushing her mouth with his. He took her to their cabin where their bodies became one under intense passion, his masterful touch causing her to blossom under him, taking him into her.

When he left, he was sombre and just stood at the rail as he watched the land mass. Rosa-Lee would watch with distress, touching her belly reassuringly.

Pierre had his hands full with both Roberto and Rosa-Lee. But it was easier to speak to her than Roberto. He shut everyone out. Pierre knew to just be there and make sure to cover his friend's back once they set foot on the island.

For three days, they sailed around the south coast and up the east coast until they reached the Isle of Saint Marie. It was a beautiful island filled with lush, thick foliage, a mountain on the far horizon.

During these three days, their lovemaking was at times frightening Rosa-Lee. It felt as if he were branding her with every touch and every kiss. There were times when he hurt her, but she didn't say anything, her trust in him unmovable. Her body was adjusting and aroused under his raw desire. The things he did with her astounded her, but it brought them closer, leaving her breathless and numb in his arms.

When he finally stepped out of the cabin after the anchor was dropped, she saw the man she had met the first day of their journey, the menacing, stern pirate. Her Roberto was deeply buried.

The longboat was set out on the water, waiting for him. She had to wait on board for him.

When he kissed her, he said, "It will be either Pierre or I that will collect you. Be ready at any time."

"Yes, Captain." She looked at him and he smiled. For a brief second, the Roberto that she loved was back as she touched his cheek. He kissed her palm and then her lips in a final good-bye.

When he went over the railing and down the Jacob's ladder, Captain Roberto de Ville was in full command of his surroundings, stern in posture, broad shoulders straight and expression fierce, the picture of a pirate.

Pierre followed he assured Rosa-Lee once again that he would protect him and bring him back safe. She squeezed his hand in a final good-bye and watched as the love of her life moved over the water without looking back.

The ship's doctor took her hand and motioned for her to go to her cabin. He had watched her the last few days and knew she did not feel well. Now was a good time to determine what was wrong although he had his suspicions. He smiled at the young woman, reassuring her that everything was all right, that Roberto knew what he was doing and that she must trust him.

It was with great difficulty that he calmed her down once his suspicions were confirmed. Rosa-Lee cried and laughed the whole of the night, staying in their cabin with the wonder that was within her. She could barely contain herself until waves of worry would capture her and create havoc in her mind.

Roberto himself had great difficulty in leaving her behind. But he had to determine if everything was still all right on the island. A pirate's life changed in minutes and he had been gone eight months. The Falcon was unpredictable on the best of days.

As they rowed to the shore, he refused to look back knowing that Rosa-Lee would watch him expectantly. But he could not afford to turn around. He had to leave her behind and think clear-headed for now. That was the difference between survival and certain death.

At the shore he was met by several men; some new ones and some familiar faces. He was rushed to the Falcon's place immediately. He hardly saw the dense bush as his eyes were fixed on the men with him, observing each one as they went deeper into the over-grown bushes. A path snaked through the trees and bushes, leaving the place dark at times.

Everyone in the group was loyal to the Falcon. The few men he knew were not among this group.

They reached an opening where several huts stood close by with a larger one in the middle. Heat emanated from the blue sky with only a slight breeze that ruffled his hair and jacket. Perspiration covered his body, but he did not notice it as he tightened his jaw.

Screams echoed from the large hut and Roberto could only guess what was going on. He hardened his features as they walked into the larger hut, larger than most on the island.

The hut had once belonged to a chieftain on the island, but Falcon had killed the man and his wives and taken his children as slaves. He was living in the place as the chief.

When they got inside the cool shadows of the large room, they saw the Falcon sitting in the middle of the room at a dining table. A woman was bend over his knee and he hit her without mercy. Several men stood around him as smacks on her bare bottom resounded through the silence. He chuckled, a deep, rough noise that came from his throat, his beady eyes dark with cruelty.

Roberto clenched his fists in anger, but he could not show it. When the Falcon noticed Roberto, he stopped the smacks.

"Are my trusted son" Falcon greeted him jovially and stood. The woman fell to the ground and he kicked her aside. "Take her away," he barked to no one in particular. Two men stepped forward and reached for her unceremoniously. She screamed. One smacked her hard and she fell backward. Her face was puffed up, her eyes swollen. She was in agony, but it did not bother the chief.

"Take her, dammit," the Falcon cursed loudly.

"What must we do with her?" a bald man asked with a grin. That was Trevor, a rogue they had picked up on the streets of London. A dangerous man.

Roberto knew him well, and the mere thought that the woman was at his mercy was devastating. Roberto looked at Pierre who stood with clenched jaw. Both men knew they could not help her.

"You can have her," Falcon said ruefully, and the man's face contorted in an ugly grin. "Thank you!"

It had to be one of the Falcon's favorites for him to even give her a second glance. What she had done to displease him they could only guess.

"No!" the woman screamed as he pulled her up by her hair, threw her over his shoulder, and walked out. For a while they could hear her begging, crying and screaming, but without any help. Tomorrow she would most likely be dead. They knew no help would come to her aid as the other man followed Trevor and the screaming woman. His lust apparent on his face.

"Roberto, I trust you are well?" the Falcon said as he stood before Roberto with a grin, scratching his chin.

"Yes, Falcon I am well," Roberto replied, giving away nothing of his feelings to Falcon and clasp his offered arm in a greeting.

"Pierre," Falcon acknowledged him briefly.

"Falcon," Pierre returned the greeting as Roberto had.

"And have you brought me the ransom?" The Falcon's dark eyes glimmering with satisfaction.

"Yes, Captain," Roberto answered.

"Well let me hear all about it!" He wrapped an arm around Roberto's neck and walked with him to the table. A pitcher with wine and glasses awaited them and a servant girl was already pouring it for them, hands shaking.

She received a slap from the Falcon and the pitcher fell from her hand and broke on the floor. Wine sloshed against his boots.

"Now look what you have done, you idiot woman. Clean it up!" He screamed. She was on her knees with a cloth in her hand that Roberto assumed was her skirt and cleaned up the mess with the Falcon still smacking her over the head.

Roberto balled his fist and tried to stand up, but Pierre stopped him and shook his head.

Roberto sat down and watched with growing hatred the abuse to the young woman. She scampered away through the door and left them alone.

Pierre was right it was not time for any heroics. Not yet.

"Well, tell, man! We are anxious to hear of your travels." The Falcon's second, Tiny Forehand, came and sat next to him. Tiny was, as his name stated, tiny, but with a sure hand that could impale a fly with one quick throw with his daggers. He kept them stashed behind his back. He was ruthless in his endeavours and vicious to any captive. If they needed information from an informant, he knew how to get it out skilfully, meticulously and with bloody results.

"As expected, Cisco Almaida was not very pleased with the ransom or the abduction," Roberto began, "but at the end he released the ransom as requested."

"And the daughter? Is she anything like Pedro said?"

"Yes." *And more.* But that did he not disclose. The Falcon's eyes peered in his for a long time and Roberto kept his eyes unwavering on him. The young woman was back with another pitcher, shaking. Before she could pour the contents, Roberto got up and took it from her.

"You were always too soft," The Falcon said as he watched the display. "The woman needs to be put in her place, but you always were the gentleman." The group laughed gruffly. Roberto did not comment but poured all the glasses and sat back, taking a sip of his own.

"So, she is in good health?"

"Yes."

"You don't offer much, Roberto. Are you hiding something?" came the low, impatient reply.

"No, Falcon." Roberto met the Falcon's glare head on. The Falcon's eyes swept between him and Pierre but neither elaborated on anything.

"How is Pedro?" Roberto asked instead, and a smug grin appeared on the Falcon's face.

"The little sneak got away. How I still don't know, but I will get to the bottom of it soon." Pierre and Roberto looked at each other briefly before they placed their attention back on him.

"When did this happen?"

"Two days ago," and he snickered, "but don't you worry, we will get him. The patrols are canvassing the island as we speak." He slapped Tiny on his small shoulders. "And then it is playtime."

This caused Tiny to smile widely displaying his empty gums, the beady eyes sparkling with glee. But he said nothing, as always.

"If you don't mind, I want to go to my hut make sure everything is acceptable so that I can join the search," Roberto said as he drank the last of his wine and got up.

"Yes, of course, but when will I meet the ransom?" Falcon asked, bringing them back to the subject at hand.

"Soon." Both he and Pierre got up and left the hut.

Nothing was said between them, but each had a grin on their faces. The plan was under way.

Soon, Falcon, both thought.

18

Two days passed before Rosa-Lee finally saw a longboat rowing towards the *Contra O Vento*.

In all this time, she had neither heard from nor seen Roberto or Pierre. She paced their cabin nervously. She was not sure what was going on, but she felt uneasy, and all the uncertainty and doubts settled in her mind. She kept thinking of all the evidence against the man she now called husband.

Her pirate.

She loved him. That much she knew.

He was not acting like the pirates her father told her about. The cruel ways of their existence were not a part of him, or of Pierre, for that matter. The two were best friends but they rarely spoke about themselves, never let her in on the bond they shared.

Then there was that letter she had delivered to the Captain of the D.E.I.C ship. Why would a pirate hand a D.E.I.C captain a letter? It did not add up.

His persistence in reminding her that she must trust him because everything was not as it seemed caused more questions. He was a pirate, strict and fierce, although she had seen a side of him that she doubted other people were privy to.

He was an exceptional lover, tender at times, brutal at other times, but he always adored her. She felt safe in his strong arms and she smiled, wrapping her arms around herself. She missed him fiercely.

His love of good books was evident. The rows of books on the shelves were worn at the corners from years of reading. His knowledge of the world astounded her. He had seen most of the known world, which she only heard from her father or had read about.

He had a love for both land and sea as he talked about the farm, the land, his country and his parents. He loved them, missed them and still talked about his sister reverently.

He knew the seas, the currents, and every kind of cloud and what it meant. He knew when to be fearful of the sky and prepared or just dismiss it and call its bluff or, as he called it, "a pout of the heavens," nothing to be afraid of.

Then there were those dreamy hands that made magic over her skin, the smile that lit up his face, causing the scar to disappear into the laugh lines, the glow of his passionate eyes when he made love with her, coaching her.

Her tender loving pirate. Her heart ached because of her unexpected love for him. It was the not knowing that drove her to pacing. Enrico kept her company the best he could, but she knew she did not make it easy for the chamber boy, hardly listening when he told of his past life before he joined Roberto's crew.

The pirate ships lying at anchor all around her unnerved her, menacing and dark, holding secrets she was sure she didn't want to know, the world of her husband.

Sometimes he would tell her stories, but she was sure he toned it down, not to upset her, but she did have a healthy imagination and she could read between the lines. After all, her father did tell them stories as well, stories that were fearful filled with terror and horror. From her father they were stories that other people lived, yet now it was different. Roberto lived them, making it all real. The scars proved that.

Then there were the women. Her husband was virile, that she knew, and to imagine him in the arms of others made her blood boil in jealousy. They had known him, enjoyed his lovemaking long before she was in the picture. They had taught him the things he was teaching her now and it did not sit well with her. She had not mentioned it to him and knew she had to work through it if she wanted to continue to trust him.

The men made sure that she stayed hidden in the cabin so as not to attract any unnecessary attention. The crew was on alert all the time. Tension hung like a thick, unseen blanket in the air. They were ready for anything, but it was not good for her nerves. The not knowing, not being out there created more nerves.

Her stomach clenched and when she woke the morning of the second day, she had to run for the chamber pot. Sweat rolled down her trembling body and the moment Enrico saw her he called for the doctor. She was pale and worn out.

The doctor encouraged her to eat often; if not for her, for the new life she carried.

As the long boat bumped against the hull Rosa-Lee finally got herself under control and went to the upper deck.

Pierre stepped on the upper deck with heavy boots and the men were glad to see him, meeting him with toothy grins. He was also a good man and the crew respected him. He had a self-assurance about him that made him attractive.

Rosa-Lee had seen loneliness in him a few times and often wondered about it, but over the past four months, he had never once spoken about himself. The same vibe that she had from Roberto she also had about him. Likewise, he did not match the description of a pirate, yet he was one. He laughed easily and was pleasant to talk to. What did they hide?

"Are you ready, Señorita?" All familiarity was gone, and they treated her like in the beginning. She had also noticed that they did not call her Señora. There must be a reason for that. She was sure it would become clear later.

"Yes, Señor, I am," she replied, stroking the dress she had chosen with care, a pale blue taffeta which enhanced her creamy neck, shoulders and bosom. The bodice was hand-stitched with fine needlework. It clung around her and she found it difficult to breathe but it gave her the necessary courage to do what was expected. Her waist was cinched small, according to the latest fashion. She patted herself on her still-flat tummy as if to remind herself what was at stake.

They helped her into the long boat. The boats man, who was unknown to her, looked at her with a lustful grin. His eyes roamed over her body and she felt shivers running down her spine. She did not meet the arrogant stare.

With precision, they rowed to land. Rosa-Lee felt small as they passed the menacing ships. Men whistled and cheered them on as they passed, but she kept her head down, cringing under some of the vulgar comments. Pierre touched her on the back, unnoticed by the rest, reminding her that he was there, and she knew she was safe with him around.

They landed and for the first time in four months, she was back on solid ground. Her legs felt unsteady and almost out of place but soon the feeling of stable firmness of the land returned and she walked steadily behind Pierre. Her eyes were on his boots.

Men watched her, following her with greedy, hungry eyes. Pierre had tied her hands together with a blank look, pulling her behind him; she said nothing, looked nowhere in particular, and made no eye contact with anyone.

Men tried to grope at her but Enrico, who walked behind her the whole time, removed their hands with ease, protecting her. Unbearable smells welled up in her nose, and she had to fight very hard against the nausea that made her want to double over. She had to swallow a few times to get it down but remained calm, willing herself to breathe controlled breaths.

After about fifteen minutes of walking through the throng, they came into a clearing. Men stood all around her, looking down at her with piercing, hungry eyes. Stifling smoke filled the air. Her eyes burned from it and Pierre left her alone, but she could sense Enrico behind her and was at ease.

She looked around, searching for the man she loved, and when she saw him between a few men, she wanted to call him. Roberto stood out tall and strong, far above them, looking at her with a blank stare as if he did not know her in this world. She remembered his words and repeated to herself, *He loves me. I know this, trust him.*

Suddenly there was a light buzz in the air and in her vision another man stepped up, large and menacing. Fierce words assaulted her.

The Falcon, she guessed. The nose was a dead giveaway to the name. He was huge, and she had to lift her head to look at him towering over her. His teeth were yellow, signalling his unhealthy lifestyle and an ugly grin was on his face. Handsome was not a word used in the same sentence with this man. He was extremely rough. His face had a leather-like look from years of exposure to the elements.

He looked at her; the grin reached his eyes but made it more sinister.

"Ah the sister, finally. Ah, but you are pretty." With rough hands he took her chin in his hand turning her head to both sides. She could not help herself and shivered.

He did not let on that he noticed it and continued,

"Your brother did not lie. You are pretty." He roared with laughter and the men joined in, except Roberto. He stood there emotionless, looking straight at her, not missing anything. Disgust filled his eyes as the pirate touched her.

"Where is my brother, you bastard?" she hissed, unwavering before the Pirate.

An overwhelming, disgusting stench came to her when he breathed directly into her face.

"Your brother will come when I am good and ready. First, I am going to play with you," he said, grabbing her breasts.

"A handful!" he said, looking at his men and laughed. A chorus of laughter followed, and she flinched, it hurt when he touched her. Anger filled her, and she stood up straight, looking him directly in the eye.

"You would like to kill me, wouldn't you, sweetheart?" he said with a smirk of defiance.

Again, a roar broke loose, men slapping their knees as they laughed.

"I am going to enjoy you. Let me have a look at you." With one swift movement, he ripped her bodice from her, exposing her to all the hungry eyes. Lips smacked. Disgust coiled within her belly, threatening to spill over her lips but she swallowed, refusing to back down.

He brushed away her hair, cupping her breasts again. Roberto fumed, clenching his fists and stepped forward. Pierre held him back.

"Slow down, friend, your time will come," he spoke softly into his ear, holding him back at his shoulder.

The Falcon came closer, looking at her with pale green eyes and investigating her skin as if she was under a searchlight. She felt humiliated, exposed to every hungry glare. The rough hands kneaded her, and he leaned forward to suckle a breast, catching the nub between his teeth so that it stretched. She flinched in pain, sniffing. He chuckled, the sound trembling through her and she clenched her fists as he continued.

Suddenly he stopped and sniffed again, and then hollered:

"I smell a man on her! You bloody bitch, you've had sex!" Enraged, he slapped her, and she fell to the ground. Her cheek burned as she struggled up and stood in defiance before him, looking at the pirate with disdain and hate. He came closer again, looking at her abdomen, and again he raged,

"She is with child!" He slapped her again so that she fell on her backside.

"I will take the bitch!" a pirate called out.

"I don't mind. The bitch will not live long enough to be a mummy," another scoffed in mockery. Again, the air filled with laughter. This time it mingled with lust as they looked at her, knowing one of them would have her that night.

Roberto shook in rage as he heard the news and for a split second a smile appeared before it was gone, keeping his face still as his Rosa lay on the ground.

An instant later she stood up straight again. Her hair fell forward and covered one breast. Her chin lifted, and his heart swelled with pride. *There are the thorns.* He had missed them. Her body was rigid as she stared the Falcon down. Her arms and bound hands drew protectively over her abdomen, the place his child grew.

It will take more than that to break her, he thought.

"Take her away!" The Falcon screamed, his eyes flashing. Out of the corner of her eye, she saw Roberto moving toward them, saying, "What do you want me to do with the bitch?"

"You can have her!" the Falcon screamed. "I wanted a virgin. Why is it so hard to find a virgin in the world, especially one that is supposed to be a lady?" he screamed.

"Thank you, Falcon," Roberto replied, bowing respectfully, grabbing her arm and pulled her away. She struggled against him and he slapped her. Her eyes spat fire as he held her. Shocked she willed him to look at her, but he ignored her.

"You pirate scum!" she hissed, but Roberto did not flinch as pirates roared behind them, calling her names.

Quickly he made way with Rosa-Lee behind him. He moved her closer to him to cover her nakedness and left the circle. Pierre and Enrico were not very far behind, hands on their swords as they watched every move from the men, every thick bush. They followed a small path leading them up the hill and at a rocky dead end, turned right into a wooden structure.

The rough wood structure was built in a huge square, standing on a wooden deck mere inches from the ground. Five steps led up to the veranda without any railings around it. The roof was shingled with dark wood. Two windows framed each side of the wooden door and on both sides, closing with shutters, no glass in the panes. As they stepped onto the wooden deck, it creaked underneath their weight. Pierre and Enrico stepped aside as he opened the door for her.

Roberto was quiet all the way to his hut. Her imagined angry words resounding in his head after he had slapped her. He had to do it. It was expected of him as the son of the Falcon, but he was furious with himself for what she had just been through. How could he face her?

When they were inside, and the door closed, Roberto stood with his back to her, closing his eyes. He was afraid of what he could see in her eyes, the rejection of what just happened. Instead, he heard her softly speak.

"We were about six months into our journey, walking through the thick dense jungle of Africa, which was a struggle in the scorching humid heat. My father had to cut a path through it, the only one with enough strength to do so. He was also hungry and very tired." He could barely hear her and imagined how she looked at him, but he could not turn, only listen.

"My mother's feet were completely giving out, as skin fell from them, leaving them a raw, bloody mess. She tried to hide it, never cried once. But when my father saw it, he was furious with her and could not believe the damage caused to them. He bandaged them with strips of his shirt under much protest from her. The sneering remarks some had made held them apart and she did not want him to be in more trouble. Father continued with the nursing of her feet and she was grateful in the end. The captain was furious, cursing him, but he ministered to her wounds and carried us both without complaint." He heard a smile in her voice, and he blinked as moisture settled in his eyelids.

"A savage tribe helped my father to get food. We thought the chief was a good man. But he indicated to my father that he wanted payment for the food and then looked at the women: my mother, my half-sister, and two slave women. Father removed all their clothing to show the chief that they were too skinny after the lack of food during that time. Father had to point out my mother and my half-sister's bony shoulders and hips to the man, only covered with skin. Father compared them to the chief's own wives, over weight and huge."

"The chief did not like skinny women and dismissed them, to great relief of the remaining group, me included. He wanted big, chubby women and showed off his own women standing behind him. The two slave girls still had enough on their bones to win his approval and they agreed without any struggle to stay behind. To them, it did not matter where they were. If they had food, they were satisfied. By then they were used to being abused and given away to whoever owned them. The two women did not even put up a fight."

She was quiet for a few minutes, as tears ran down her face, her cheeks swollen and sensitive, but bravely she continued, and he swallowed at the tears that ran down his face.

"First you married me and then you branded me so that he could smell you on me. The past week making love to me, you branded me so hard that at times it hurt, but you saved me, didn't you?" He turned around, tears rolling down his cheeks, and she walked into his open embrace, looking at him with trust and love.

He did not deserve her.

"I said I would trust you, no matter what." And she comforted him, his head on her shoulder.

"I am so sorry that you had to go through that, but that was the only way that I could protect you. You were so brave, my Rosa." His touch on her cheek stung after the slaps. With both his hands, he cupped her face and kissed her, his breath warm against her skin. Then, jerking his head up, he asked curiously,

"Are you with child?"

"Yes I am. The doctor confirmed it two days ago, and I wanted to surprise you."

He lifted her in the air, twirling her around, laughter in his voice.

"I am going to be a father!"

"Yes, you are, my love," she laughed, her cheeks still hurting. He put her down and with a warm hand enclosed her stomach in wonderment, removing the restraints and the rest of her clothing, kneeling in front of her.

"Your mama is the most gorgeous and the bravest woman you will ever know, little one," he whispered into her tummy, his lips brushing against her skin as his hands held her hips.

She knelt in front of him with love pure and unstrained, eyes dark with desire.

"Make love to me," she whispered.

"How can I refuse that request?" He brought her closer, their lips locked in tenderness.

"I love you, my Rosa." He crushed her body against his, demanding her mouth. With hunger he devoured her. She removed his clothing, struggling to get to the bed.

When they finally did manage to get there, he became tender in his love. Whispering tender words in her ear, on her stomach, the vibrancy of every word causing her to arch into him. She demanded his attention, but he continued with the slow torture until she pleaded for him to end the sweet torture. He just ignored her and continued at his own pace, deliberate in every lingering touch.

19

It took him awhile to sleep, with his pregnant wife in his arms, just holding her as if his life depended on it. Kissing her softly, he smiled when she sighed in his arms, deep in sleep, cuddling into him, her body draped over him.

The strength and bravery she showed the previous day; then the understanding she showed for his actions, made him feel like a real man. She trusted him. His chest swelled under her head, her hair fanning over his body, covering them like a blanket.

He knew he could have a future with her and his child growing inside of her. It was the greatest gift he had ever received, unconditional love for a rough pirate feared by many.

She was worth it. To fight for their future was worth everything.

Thinking of the story she had told, he had admitted that he respected Cisco Almaida as a man and as a father. Clearly Rosa-Lee had great admiration for him, as all her stories always involved him. He would have to thank the man once he took her back, for he had prepared her for him without knowing him. He smiled as she stretched her body against him. Her hand moved over him in a caress and his body reacted to the soft, gentle touch. He rolled her on her back and made love to her in the sweetest way. The soft womanly smile he received let him grin with pleasure, knowing that she enjoyed it as much as he enjoyed giving it.

During the night they both woke simultaneously. Moonlight streamed in through the shutter slats so that they could make out anything inside. Something had woken them and when Roberto looked out, he could see a shadow passing under the door. He pointed to the door and whispered in her ear to get up quickly and quietly. They stood up and dressed.

Again, she put on her brother's clothing and when Roberto looked at her with dismay, she shrugged her shoulders without saying a word. She figured this would be the best way to move on the island and the safest. When she had packed a bag, these were the only clothing she had taken, along with her knife and pistol. She slipped them into the belt under the jacket and grabbed a sword to belt under the jacket.

The dress on the floor was torn; the fabric stretched and damaged. She had no need for that dress.

In the back corner of the wooden structure was a trap door that he lifted. They went through it quickly and he closed the door behind him. He motioned for her to go out and stay in the bushes close by. He wanted to see what was going on at the front door. After a few minutes, he returned, speaking into her ear.

"There is no sign of Pierre or Enrico. We will have to get away from here. Follow me." He took her hand. They ducked through dense bushes, past another few wooden structures until they reached a clearing, they could hear a soft sobbing sound. Rosa-Lee pointed it out to Roberto who nodded his head. She moved forward toward the sounds.

A young girl stood crying behind a tree. Shadows played over the face. The moonlight was not bright enough through the canopy, but she could see that the young girl was in distress.

"Don't be afraid," Rosa-Lee said softly. "We are here to help you." The girl stopped crying, sniffing.

"What is your name?" Rosa-Lee whispered in her ear, putting a hand on her arm.

"Nora."

"Why are you here?"

"I was captured from the coast of Mozambique. They brought me on a ship this afternoon. The moment I got a chance, I slipped away from the pirate who kept me in his hut."

Rosa-Lee looked at Roberto. "We cannot leave her here. She has to come with us."

"As long as she does not hold us up," he whispered.

"I will not. Please, take me with you," came the desperate plea.

They heard movement behind them, as people came closer. Quickly, they introduced themselves to the young girl.

"Nora, I am Rosa-Lee, and this is Roberto. Follow us." She took the girl's hand in her own, clutching it tightly.

They continued until they reached the shoreline, close to a longboat lying on the beach.

"Get in," said Roberto and started to push. Nora was already at the edge when they were stopped.

"Not so fast, Roberto," a stern voice said from behind them. They turned around and behind them stood the Falcon, rigid and fierce and three of his men equally menacing, a torch in each one's hand lit the beach around them.

Rosa-Lee and Roberto drew their swords, ready. The Falcon walked closer, straight to Rosa-Lee, looked at her, and said, "Who have we here?" Reaching toward her, he lifted the torch to her face and smirked.

"Ah, Señorita, lovelier than ever, I almost did not recognize you in men's clothing." He cupped her cheeks again.
Her heart was racing as she slapped his hand away, lifting her sword.

"Leave her alone!" Roberto said sternly.

"You really care about this bitch, son. You deceived me. It took me awhile to see through your plan but now I am back to claim her. She will be mine."

"No!" screamed Rosa-Lee and launched forward. The point of the sword tore a hole in the Falcon's black shirt.

"Ouch! You bitch, you scratched me," he said in surprise.

Roberto moved forward, in between them, his sword drawn, anger in his voice and eyes.

"You will not touch her again, Falcon. I will kill you."

The Falcon laughed, drawing out his sword.

"Let's see if you can." Both men knew each other's strength. Both knew they had the same cunning and skill to win. Both had a roguish grin on their faces.

They circled each other. Rosa- Lee moved the young girl behind her, her eyes on the other three standing close by, swords drawn, menacing faces snarling at them.

Soon you could hear the clash of steel upon steel resounding at a high pitch through the night. Swiftly both the men moved on the ground, feet trained and steady on the loose sand, cutting into the air, stabbing towards each other with short body blows. Roberto cut the Falcon's shoulder and then his abdomen with one sweep, hardly wounded, a defiant smirk on his face.

"You son of a bitch," the Falcon screamed, throwing himself at Roberto.

Roberto stepped gracefully to the side and landed another blow to Falcon's face. Blood streamed from the Falcon's wounds, down his leg, into the sand. The younger man clearly had the upper hand.

Then one of the other men stepped closer, launching at Roberto with an angry growl, Roberto reacted and diverted the blow, cutting into the man's arm. His sword sank deep into the flesh. The man cried out, grabbing his arm in disbelief, storming with fury towards Roberto. Roberto sidestepped again, punching the man in the face.

He fell to the ground as the Falcon moved forward again. Cutting into the air, weariness on his face, he launched forward onto Roberto's sword.
Grabbing the sword, his face was stunned. "You wounded me, you son of a bitch!" he fell on his knees.

Another man screamed, running into Roberto. The last one made a lunge at Rosa-Lee, but she cut him, blood dripping from the sword point. She waited for him as he moved forward again. She protected her face with her sword, pushing him away from her with both hands, and then she attacked without uttering a word. Her sword disappeared into the man's chest.

Nora screamed and covered her mouth with a hand, trembling in fear.

Glassy eyes looked at Rosa-Lee as the man fell backward on the sand. Waves covered him, pulling him farther out to sea. However, Rosa-Lee did not notice and turned back to the fighting behind her.

Roberto fought against the two men and he fell as a blow struck his head. A stream of blood ran down his face and the Falcon came for him. Roberto managed to strike the sword away from him. He was on his feet again and again steel clanked against steel.

Rosa-Lee stepped forward, covering his back with hers, and with fierce blows to both the pirates, they struck them, falling on their knees from the impact.

More men rushed forward, and the Falcon yelled, "Get them!"

One man grabbed Nora, holding his sword under her chin. Fear filled her eyes, but no sound came out. Rosa-Lee and Roberto stopped in mid-lunge as the sound of a catching breath resonated in the air. Looking at Nora, they lowered their swords.

"Seize them!" the Falcon yelled again. "Take them to the tavern."

Their swords were taken, and the Falcon came closer, punching Roberto on the cheek. His ring cut through the skin and a trickle of blood dripped from his face.

"Your bitch has killed one of my men!" Looking at Rosa-Lee with a hateful glare he vowed, "She will pay; he was one of my best!"

"Clearly not," Rosa-Lee said with a menacing smile.

He walked over to her and slapped her so hard that her head bounced back, slamming into the man who held her.

When her gaze returned to the Falcon she said in a very cold voice, "I will kill you." She pronounced each word in clipped tones, her promise unmistakable.

He grabbed her shirt and pulled her up to face him directly. The other man let go his hold and he tied her hands in front of her. His eyes spat angry blue flames, shoving her toward the lights in the distance. She remained on her feet and the group walked away, Nora still in the clutches of the other man.

When they reached the tavern, they were tied up together. A huge crowd formed around them. Soft sobs came from Nora. Rosa-Lee could see her for the first time. She was small and blond, not as young as she thought, but with beautiful blue eyes.

Weariness and the day's hardships were visible on her. Her dress was torn and filthy. It looked like she had been dragged at one point. She was full of scratch marks on her lower arms. Her feet were bare and bloody.

"Roberto, my son," the Falcon said with a snarl in his voice, mocking him with the endearing word.

"Did you really think that you would get rid of me this easily? I have watched you for a while now. You were up to something. I could see that. You took the woman that was meant for me and made her your wife, planting your seed in her to make you a daddy. How touching. You thought I would not know?" He slapped him hard. Roberto's head snapped back, his ears ringing. He returned his gaze, hate smouldering in the depths.

"A pirate with a wife, what a laugh!" Roars of boisterous laughter filled the place and goblets slammed together. Mocking could be heard all over, the men parroting their leader. "Playing daddy!" They doubled over.

"And then you steal another slave from one of my men. Are you going to marry her too?" Again, a roar of laughter.

"You are the one that made sure that Pedro escaped. I don't know when or how, but you will pay for that as well." The Falcon stood before Roberto looking him directly in the eye, spit hanging from his beard.

"You have cost me a lot and I will collect from you and this bitch." He turned to Rosa-Lee.

"My men saw your brother at Santa Apollonia. I am waiting for their return as we speak. Then both brother and sister will squeal like pigs after we had our way with them. Both are so pretty, don't you think?"

"What are you waiting for, Falcon, here I am!" Pedro's strong young voice reached their ears and Rosa-Lee's face broke out in shocked surprise and grinned. To see her younger brother was truly a big relief. He stood there, equally rigid, his young body straight, his face stern and determined. At that moment she knew how her father looked at that age. Pride filled her heart.

The Falcon whirled around in surprise and the snarl disappeared from his menacing face, before it returned in mocking confidence.

Her heart beat increased, trying to make sense of the new development. With Pedro was a big, dark man who matched Pedro in size and height, but looked older.

"Pedro!" Rosa-Lee screamed with pure joy when she saw him and laughed.

"Shut up!" The Falcon slapped her again and she fell under the onslaught.

"You better stop that," she seethed, struggling to reach for him. "I am tired of you slapping me. Unfasten me and fight me, you coward!" So infuriated was she with the man in front of her, she did not notice the buzz and then the silence.

"Rosa-Lee, calm down and look," Roberto said to her softly. Men in uniform filled the tavern as the big man walked closer, his eyes fixed on the Falcon.

"I am Captain le Roux and I am here to arrest you, Falcon, you and your men." He tossed a rolled paper to him.

"Consider yourself served, you and your brood of vipers, as you deserve, by hanging." His voice echoed in the silence. There was no room for argument and for a brief second, a pin could be heard before a huge fight broke loose between the uniforms and the pirates.

Roberto managed to free his hands and when he looked up, Pierre was standing close to him, in battle with two men. He untied Rosa-Lee and Nora, who sank to the ground in exhaustion. He did not notice the pure hatred in Rosa-Lee's eyes as they set on the Falcon, the man who had caused all of this. The moment Roberto released her she sprang into action.

Rosa-Lee grabbed a dagger from the ground and launched at the Falcon, who grinned at her. With one fierce blow to his heart, she killed him. It was so swift that it did not even register with him as he fell to the ground, the same grin on his face.

Before Roberto could react, she had sprung away from him, and an instant later stood over the lifeless body of the Falcon, staring at the pirate's lifeless eyes.

He stepped closer to her and spoke, not to alarm her.

"My Rosa it is over, give me the dagger," he said into her ear, stroking her arm to calm her. For the first time since the ordeal began, she turned, pressed herself into him, and cried.

Her body shook with sobs and he stroked her back, whispering soft words in her ear while the fighting continued around them.

Pedro came over to them, climbing over the lifeless body, and reached for his sister.

"Rosa-Lee, my sister," he said in a thick, raspy voice. The emotions were too much for brother and sister. She left Roberto's arms and threw herself into his. With a satisfied grin,

Roberto left them to be reunited once again. Her brother was safe, and she kissed him all over the face as renewed tears rolled from her eyes. She clutched his shoulders.

"You are safe, Pedro!"

"Yes sister."

"I love you."

"I love you too." He hugged her, pulled her away and smiled. "I cannot believe you are here. Just look at you!"

She smiled, wiping tears from her face. "You don't look so bad yourself," she said. And they both laughed, releasing all the pent-up emotions from the last few months.

After a while, Roberto returned to her side and she stepped into his waiting arms, holding her again after he helped Pierre, killing the one man with his sword. All the pirates were finally apprehended and tied up.

"Pedro, I want you to meet my husband, Roberto de Ville," she announced with pride. Pedro looked at her then at Roberto. He clapped his new brother-in-law on the shoulder.

"Well done, sir."

Rosa-Lee looked at him, then at Roberto. "Sir?" Pedro grinned.

"You, my sister, are looking at the brave Roberto de Ville, Captain in the Dutch East India Company."

"Roberto?" she gasped. He grinned.

"You are not a pirate?" she asked, bewildered.

"No, my Rosa. I am an honest member of the working society."

She wrapped her arms around him with a soft scream of delight and kissed him fiercely to the delight of all present.

Pedro chuckled and left them. He liked the man. He would be a good husband to her.

††††

Pierre was tying up the men he had bested and saw the small body with her head bowed. Long blond tresses covered the face and he wondered who it was. Handing the men over to an officer, he walked over to the young blond girl unmoving on the floor, too drained to be interested in the activities around her. He touched her lightly on the shoulder. She looked up. Two pairs of bright blue eyes met, the one very shy and scared, the other full of interest.

Holding out a hand, he helped her to her feet gallantly. He could see that she was distressed, tears running down her face. He gave her his handkerchief, which she took with a small, delicate hand, whispering a "Thank you." Not sure what to expect, she dropped her eyes, still scared with everything that had happened. She shivered from cold and weariness and he gathered her closer, supplying her with much-needed warmth, feeling the fear and tension leaving her body. She was so small that he had to bend over to hold her, but for some reason it felt good. She fitted right into him.

"Are you all right, Señorita?" he asked with concern.

She nodded. "Yes, Señor. I just do not understand what is going on. Does this mean that I am free?" Again, the blue eyes met his with hope and trust in their depths and his heart skipped a beat.

"Yes, Señorita, it means you are free. The D.E.I.C came to our rescue."

"Who are you, Señor?"

"My name is Pierre du Val, Captain in the Dutch East India Company." He bowed before her with a gorgeous smile.

"And who am I addressing?"

She blushed. "Nora Denhaag," she replied and curtseyed, lifting the hem of her skirt. The sight of her bloody foot dismayed Pierre greatly. He crouched down and examined one foot and then the other.

"It is not that bad, Señor, just some scratches."

"Are you sure, Señorita?"

"Yes I am." He tried to determine whether she spoke the truth and she smiled shyly, dropping her skirt over her feet.

"Would you like to sit down?" He rose to his full height, towering over her.

"No, thanks, I think if I sit down I will fall asleep. I am tired." Pierre looked around, not sure what to do with her, but he wanted to spend more time with her. Everyone was still busy with the pirates and a thought occurred to him. He pondered for a few seconds.

"Would you like to stroll down the beach with me, Señorita Nora?" He held out an arm and she looped her arm through his, smiling up to him. Dimples appeared on each cheek and Pierre was mesmerized, lost.

"Yes, kind Señor," she chuckled. "I would love that."

20

Out of breath, Rosa-Lee pushed Roberto away, her eyes full of questions, surprised, confused. Roberto smiled at the mixed emotions on her face, still holding onto his brave wife.

"What would you like to know?"

"There are a million questions racing through my mind. I don't know where to begin," she replied. "I am so surprised. How…? When…? Where…? I do not know. Start at the beginning, I guess." Rosa-Lee asked, stammering, not sure what to say.

"Would you like to sit down? It could take a while?"

"Yes, and I need water. I am terribly thirsty."

"I will get you some." He left her arms to draw a pitcher closer with some wine in it. Sniffing at the contents, he found it drinkable and handed it to her. All around them lay broken pitchers. It was a wonder this one was still intact. She raised it to her mouth and took small sips. Sitting next to her, with her hand in his, Roberto began at the beginning.

"I already told you my sister and I were sold to pay off the debt for my father, and how I became the Falcon's son." She nodded.

"I was captured by the D.E.I.C about a year after my adoption for minor crimes. I made a deal with them that I would hand them Falcon on a platter if they would give me a break. After much negotiation, they gladly accepted the offer. They made me first a lieutenant and then later a captain, because I handed them another well-known pirate." He smiled at her and her eyes were fixed on him.

"The Falcon was a bastard by anyone's standards and was slipping through their fingers each time, creating havoc wherever he went. The idea of kidnapping you was born the moment I met Pedro, when we captured the merchant ship for loot. Pedro was impressive, to say the least. The Falcon was also impressed with him. When he learned whose ship we had looted, he immediately started to talk to him, having admired your father all his life. I send a letter to the HQ informing them of the new development, and they gave me permission to recruit Pedro. Together we devised the plan, giving it as a suggestion to the Falcon to get more money in the coffers. Of course, it had to be subtle so that he would think he came up with the plan, and when he finally gave the order, we were ready. We made sure Alfonso was out of harm's reach before I left to get you."

"But how did Pedro "escape"?"

"When we arrived back on the island, Pedro was already gone. I searched for him all over the island. That is why I left you on the ship so long, for your protection. I was not sure what was going on."

"I missed you," she pouted.

"I missed you, too." He smiled as he kissed her pouty lips.

Captain le Roux came to the couple with questioning brows. Rosa-Lee looked at him and then at Roberto, expecting that he would be arrested, the truth still new to her, but instead, the big man smiled at Roberto and said,

"My friend, finally I see you again after all these months. I received your letter from Captain Peek du Toit."

"My friend," Roberto said and then turned to Rosa-Lee. "Let me introduce you to my wife, Rosa-Lee de Ville."

"Señora, what an honour. Captain du Toit was very impressed with you. We thank you for the letter and your bravery. You do your father proud."

With her heart soaring, she smiled at the man she called husband, safely wrapped in his arms. All this time, he had asked her to trust him, telling her that all was not as it seemed, and with a foolish heart she did, scolding herself. But now all was clear, and she sighed in contentment, dropping her head on his shoulder, just drinking him in.

"I am so glad that Captain de Ville has found happiness with you, my dear. It does us all good."

"But how?" she asked, remembering something. "He was really adopted by the Falcon?"

"Yes, it is true. I recruited him ten years ago as an agent after he came to us with information. Your brother is also working for us. This was all a plan to capture the Falcon for his misdeeds throughout the years. Roberto stayed and gathered all the evidence for the Falcon's day in court, but it took a lady to bring him down." Captain le Roux laughed at her disbelief, looking at the lifeless body of the Falcon.

"Did Roberto not tell you?"

She could only shake her head and then looked at her husband with brand new eyes, love visible in the hazel depths. Roberto placed a kiss on her nose with a conceited smile. He was proud of this woman. She had married him for the man he was and not the title he wore. The title of pirate placed fear in most, but not her. He hugged her.

Rosa-Lee turned to her brother, who had returned to her not as a child, but as a young man. Proudly, he stood there smiling at her.

"Hi, sister," Pedro said sheepishly.

"Papa will be so proud," she whispered, and he grinned with delight.

"I recruited him when I met him ten months ago," Roberto said with pride in his voice.

"He reminds me a lot of you, the same courage and persistence. But you definitely are more beautiful." She blushed, the look on her husband's face telling her what he really wanted to do.

"Roberto, why didn't you tell me? Your secret would have been safe with me."

"It was better this way," he replied, smiling, removing a wisp of hair from her forehead.

"That is why you wanted me to trust you so much, and now I am glad I did. You are a wonderful man, and I love you very much."
She pulled him closer, kissing him in front of everyone. The arousal she sensed in him made her forget everyone else.

Pierre and Nora strolled away down to the beach. Everywhere pirates were either running or fighting the D.E.I.C soldiers, but each one was successfully captured by them and tied up. Men cursed as they were led away, giving no second glance to the young couple.

"But are you not a pirate?" she asked, seeing the commotion around her. Pierre had managed to get her a pair of shoes to protect her feet, but she was flopping in them. They were three sizes too big for the delicate feet scuffing next to him, breaking the silence with every step, causing a few giggles and chuckles from them both.

"I only pretended to be one. Roberto and I were both undercover." She looked at him puzzled, and he explained. "The man who helped you with Rosa-Lee." She giggled again. Everything had happened so fast that her head was still spinning, but Pierre took his time. "We worked undercover for the last eight years on various lootings. I saved his life and offered my services on the same day. That is how we met. Since then, we have become good friends."

"You are very brave, Captain."

Pierre grinned. "And you, Señorita, are very beautiful."

A blush appeared on Nora's face. As they stopped on the white sands, the midday sun warmed their bodies. He stepped closer, brushing the long blond tresses with his fingers. Soft, silky strands flowed through them and he watched as they fell on her shoulder, her dishevelled look still appealing to his eyes. Pierre had waited a long time to find a woman he was interested in. Since he laid his eyes on the little blond, he was exceptionally interested. She turned his insides into crashing waves and he wanted to know if the feeling was mutual.

"Very beautiful." He swallowed. "May I kiss you, Señorita?" he whispered, just above the crashing of the waves. She leaned in and offered her lips without saying a word. He brushed against her plum lips, sighing in contentment.

I am going to court her. It is a long way back. Lots of time to know Nora Denhaag. His mouth tasted her sweetness, as she pressed against him, soft and fitting into his frame.

Perfect.

†††

"What is next for you?" Captain le Roux asked the next morning, after the hanging of the remaining pirates just after dawn.

"I am officially giving my resignation. I am going to be a farmer from now on. I am finished with this life. It was too long," Roberto said, looking at Rosa-Lee and then at the captain, his voice filled with seriousness, leaving no room for any doubt.

"There is something you need to know Roberto, about your parents," Captain le Roux said.
"Yes?"

"Your father passed away six months ago, and your mother four months ago. They both came down with the fever. I only received the news three months ago. I am sorry, Roberto. There is a neighbour looking after the place, awaiting your return."

A silence fell among them and Rosa-Lee reached for her husband. She knew how much he had wanted to see his parents again, and now they were both gone. It was devastating news for him. He blinked his eyes as moistness formed and bowed his head for a second.

"I have found the will that your father left. You receive everything, of course, and with it there is a letter from him to you."

The Captain handed two letters over to him. He had to walk away as he read the letter from his father. Standing at the corner of the tavern, he inhaled deeply at the gravity of not being able to see them again. It was a short letter. His father was not one to mince words. It told him how much they had missed him. The handwriting was shaky with some words blurred but he managed to read it with a sober expression.

How he had missed these two people over the years. He now knew he would never see them again. He would miss their wisdom, their love for the land that he had shared. He would never share with them his return, his newfound love, being a father. A tear ran down his face, which he wiped away, reliving the good times in his mind.

When he turned back, his emotions were under control and he spoke. "Thank you, Captain, for everything you did for them." He shook Captain le Roux's hand firmly.

"Your farm is waiting for you; for you and your wife. Go and claim it!" he slapped Roberto on the shoulder.

"You have our blessing. You have done a lot for us over the years. There will be, of course, a bonus included in your pay. Everything else you can keep," he said smiling at him.

"Thanks, Captain." He wrapped his wife in his arms. This was his life and his family. He kissed her solemnly.

21

Pierre was made the new Captain of the *Contra O Vento*. It seemed that Cisco had been informed of the new arrangements by letter and, according to the captain, was pleased that his ship would be used in future endeavours, still under the cover of a protector of his merchant ship.

Pierre and Nora were smitten with each other, walking along the beach just talking about everything, holding hands.

Nora was happy about his new assignment and told him as much, enjoying the young Captain's closeness and tenderness since they met. The moment they kissed the first time, she knew this was the man for her and she was not shy in her affections for him.

Pierre knew this was the woman for him, even if she was very young. He spent as much time with her as propriety dictated, not that there was any one that would scold him, but his mother raised him to treat a lady right and it came naturally with her. Nevertheless, the biggest thing on his mind was that he had to be convinced when he proposed to her that she would be content with him being on the sea, away from her for long months.

She would stay on the farm with his mother and sister during the long months he would be away. He told her all about the land near Lyon and the life they led there. The life of a sea captain was hard and lonely for any man, but when a loving wife waits, it makes it all worthwhile.

It took her two days to think about it, talking to Rosa-Lee and Roberto, seeking advice from them. Rosa-Lee asked her one question: "What does your heart tell you?" Then and there and she knew, returning with a positive answer. Pierre was ecstatic about her answer, twirling her around in the air to the delight of everyone. That night they celebrated under the bright moon and starry sky, people laughing and eating. When he returned her to her hut, he had a difficult time leaving her, but he wanted to do right by her.

They stayed on the island for a week to recover and restock food and water. In that time Roberto showed Rosa-Lee around the island. She saw all his favorite spots overlooking the sea from different angles and found the natives interesting. Their nights were filled with bliss and he took her in his arms and loved her without any pressure or lingering uncertainty.

Pierre returned Nora to Mozambique where she had been abducted. Nora was the daughter of a Dutch landowner, and they went to ask for permission for their marriage before they would set sail to France. They arrived one night during a festival her father celebrated for her mother.

Roberto and Rosa-Lee accompanied them on the journey, getting to know the new country and buying beautiful pieces of furniture for their home.

They spent a week with Nora's family, who were relieved and glad that she was alive and well. Her mother, Truida, had been in such a state of distress through all the time her daughter was missing, and her father had a hard time consoling his wife.

Her father, Geert, and Pierre had long talks about his life on the open sea. He had to convince her father that he was the right man for her. Though he would be gone on long voyages, Pierre assured him that Nora would be in safe hands. His mother and sister would look after her.

The marriage ceremony was performed at the parent's estate, to the great delight of her mother, who went all out, creating the perfect wedding within a week, a record for any mother.

That night he made love to her for the first time, banishing from her memory the brutality she had experienced at the hands of her pirate captor. When she relaxed with him she blossomed under his loving attention, giving herself to the man she loved in an orgasmic euphoria. For two days, they were not seen as Pierre indulged himself in the little lady with the heated passion.

Nora was a well-bred lady who, after the ordeal and in his tender care, became a vibrant young woman. Pierre loved every moment with her. Her love for the land and its people was evident when she showed him the estate. Her knowledge was vast and full of wit. He knew he had made the right choice. His mother would love her dearly. She could entertain him, playing the piano masterfully, and made him feel like the luckiest man alive.

They laughed easily, enjoying life in general and were a beautiful couple. Her mother was at ease when Nora left with her new husband.

Pedro gave Rosa-Lee a letter to their parents explaining all the events, and his employment with the D.E.I.C. with the promise that he would see them soon.

He had turned into a responsible, hard-working man that loved the sea, a man her father would be proud of.

Captain Alfonso was found with their father's merchant ship, healthy and with a toothless grin. The D.E.I.C. hid him away so that the Falcon could not find him. When Rosa-Lee saw him, she cried for joy, flinging herself into the older man's arms. He patted her on the back, assuring her that he was fine. She thought that he had also fallen under the sword of the pirates and was greatly relieved when he joined them on route to Portugal.

Soon all were on the deck of the Almaida merchant ship, heading back to Portugal. The group was excited about their new lives awaiting them, but Roberto had to admit to himself that he dreaded meeting his new father-in-law. What kind of reception would he receive from Cisco Almaida?

They had not met under the best of circumstances. He had kidnapped the man's daughter right under his nose. How would he react to their bonding as a married couple?

Looking at his sleeping wife, he stroked the protruding belly with a big calloused hand, a contented smile a permanent fixture on his face now. The scar was part of his attractiveness and not fierce-looking at all.

He loved her. There was no doubt in his mind but meeting this brave man he had heard of so many times made him worry. What if he did not accept him as her husband?

Could he really live without his Rosa? There was just no way he could. He scowled, and he pulled her closer, leaning over the sleeping form and kissing her, demanding attention from her sleepy form. With a sigh, she opened her warm mouth.
He covered her with his body, desperately searching for her, and in a daze, she realized something was wrong, a reminder of the days before they had met the Falcon. Since then she had gotten

235

used to her very tender husband and she pushed him back softly, not to alarm him. Her eyes blinked in the dark to take him in and she whispered,

"Hey, what is wrong?" He did not answer, and just consumed her more with his heated desire, and although he stoked the same feelings within her, something was not right.

"Roberto." She tried again, out of breath. "Tell me," she urged him, and he looked at her with sad eyes. He bent his head low over her body again, demanding her, and she thought it best to comply, allowing him to brand her with his lips and body like those days at sea. An all-consuming passion sizzled in the air, fogging their minds and the world out there, until there were only their bodies connecting in a euphoric bliss.

When they finally came down, back on the soft mattress, wrapped in each other's arms, trying to get in control of their breathing, she looked up into the gorgeous face and asked once again,

"What is bothering you, Roberto?"

He looked at her with dark piercing eyes, tracing her spine with a finger.

"It is nothing." He tried to shrug it away.

"No, it is not. Come on, tell me." She started to tickle him between the two ribs, a spot she knew by now. He was ticklish, and he grinned, grabbing her hand to stop her. She chuckled.

"You don't play fair," he pouted.

"Well, are you going to talk to me?" She rose, leaning on her elbow, all her attention fixated on him. He looked away, avoiding the piercing eyes. She turned his face back to her, cuddling into him with a leg over him.

"I am scared of losing you," he finally admitted, and she gasped

"Why? I plan to stick to you like barnacles on the hull of the ship. I'm going nowhere."

He knew this was stupid to think like this, but he could not help it and the dread came out as a hoarse, croaking sound.

"Your father ..." He lifted his eyes, filled with dread and terror instead of his normal stern expression. "He will hate me."

Dumbfounded, she looked at him, her lips parted in a gasp, and she lifted herself on top of him.

"Do you really think that?"

"Yes, I do." She looked away, not sure what to think. She had thought about her parent's reaction during this time and what they would think of the union. They would be shocked and surprised, but they would not hate him. They might be angry, but they would not chase him away. She turned her gaze back to him and laid a hand on the scarred cheek, beautiful and full of character.

"They will never chase you away," she whispered. "They would trust my judgment and when they see that I truly love you, they will love you." Leaning closer, she kissed his eyes and face tenderly, with words lingering between each kiss.

"You are an amazing man and my father will see that and love you," She continued. "He might be angry for a day, but he will love you." She sat up straight, lifting her leg over him and straddled him, cupping his face.

"I cannot believe my big pirate who is scared of nothing is fearful of meeting the in-laws," she giggled, and he grinned at her remark, but also at the perfect view he had of her.

"My mother will adore you. My other brother may challenge you, but he will like you." He wrapped his arms around her body, her long flowing hair curtaining them in.

"You are silly to think this way."

"Your father is Cisco Almaida. Even the Falcon admired the man, and I kidnapped you out of his house, insulted him. If it was me, I would shoot me." She placed a finger on his lips.

"He will not shoot you, Roberto. He is loving and caring, everything you are as well. He will understand." She placed another kiss on his plump lips.

"He is brave and caring and not a hard, careless man. You will see." she began straddling him with her enticing hips and he groaned softly.

"You are a temptress."

"You taught me, so don't complain."

"I know." he said and captured her mouth seductively.

22

The rest of the voyage was uneventful, if you call morning sickness between two women uneventful. Rosa-Lee's morning sickness increased right after they started on their trip to Portugal and Nora followed a month later. The men were extremely careful around them. The sea's continuous movement and the women's conflicting moods were tiresome, but they could not avoid the smiles of satisfaction in the private knowledge that they would be fathers soon, an idea neither had considered possible.

Sometimes just to get out of the cabins the men would flee to the bridge where they would talk man stuff. The men laughed at their expense, knowing the time they had was not always perfect.

Rosa-Lee tried very hard to control herself, but the whole voyage had her nerves as tight as a drum. She felt sweaty and gigantic even though she knew. It was not true and Roberto assured her he still loved her, all of her. She was not convinced, and to make matters worse, when she did not retch it out, she ate as if for an army, the hunger a permanent resident within her swollen body.

Her clothes were long outgrown. The seams had been let out until nothing remained. All she was comfortable in was Roberto's shirts, but that meant she could not go out, which was frustrating in the stifling cabin. Not that Roberto complained about less to get rid of when he wanted to cuddle into her.

Nora had it a bit better but not much. She was not growing at such a gigantic pace as Rosa-Lee. Her dresses still fit in a way, giving her more movement on the upper deck. Her morning sickness lasted longer so that by the time she had her wits about her, she was famished. But then seasickness would set in and the doctor filled his days controlling it. The cook baked special biscuits in the hopes that it would help. Some days it was fine, other days nothing stayed down, and she cried, which frustrated Pierre tremendously, just holding her the best he could, with a handsome smile.

During those times, the two friends would stay on the bridge, giving their full attention to the ship, the maps and everything else happening. But the trip was calm, with no real adventure to take their minds from their wives, consoling each other, looking miserable themselves. Now and then, the women would calm down and be the sweet women they loved and adored, only to chase them out again in anger.

After four months of rolling seas, steady winds in the sails and beautiful weather they saw land beautifully edged on the horizon. They hugged each other in relief and the men joked with them, seeming unmoved. They watched the land coming closer with every passing hour.

Again, dread filled Roberto's mind, wondering for the umpteenth time how he would be received. After that one time, he never spoke to Rosa-Lee about it again, but the nagging question remained in his head and he clenched his teeth as he looked at the unfolding land mass before him.

As the busy harbour came into view, he felt his shoulders tense and his rigid posture as stiff as a plank.

Pierre noticed his friend and former captain's tense posture and touched him on the shoulder.

"You will be fine Roberto. You are making it too much of an issue. If what Rosa-Lee is telling us is any indication of who this man is, he will accept you."

Dark eyes turned to him and he gave a tense grin. His lips were stretched and even underneath the tanned skin Pierre could see his friend was pale.

"Yes, I hear you, my friend."

"Relax." Pierre squeezed his shoulder once again.

"There you are, Roberto, love," Rosa-Lee called out, the smile on her face radiant but tired, her body uncomfortably large as she held her back. Roberto turned to look at her with tender love, softening the tensed features immediately.

"Were you looking for me, Rosa?" He welcomed her body into his arms.

"Yes love, I was wondering when we will dock?" She looked past him to the busy harbour. Large merchant ships lay in the overcrowded harbour, busy unloading or loading and they could see people scurrying around in the distance, too far away to identify.

"Not long now. By nightfall we will be there, and I will send someone to your father's place to come and get us," he replied, wrapping her in his arms and kissing her cheek.

Nora also joined them and together the two couples watched the harbour coming closer. True to his word, by the time supper was served they had found a place and could send one of the men

241

with a note to her father's house, notifying them of their arrival and requesting a carriage.

Two hours later, the boatswain announced the arrival of Cisco Almaida and Pierre went outside to meet the hero.

"Love, you need to relax," Rosa-Lee said softly, touching his thigh as he came to his feet, and he nodded, feeling animated in his actions as he helped his wife from her chair, her cheeks glowing with excitement to see her father.

The moment the dining room's door opened, and Cisco Almaida stepped, in Roberto de Ville stepped back, his eyes fixed on the giant in front of him. For the first time Roberto really looked at the man, three inches taller than himself. Cisco roared out to Rosa-Lee, who gave a jubilant yelp and disappear in the big man's chest.

"Papa," she said, "I have missed you," as bubbles of laughter burst from her and a beautiful smile adorned her face, looking up to the man who had raised her as his own.

"I have missed you, my Rosie." Roberto thought he was going to break her in two as his strong arms wrapped around the protruding belly of his pregnant wife. A smile appeared on Roberto's face. His wife's joy filled him, and he eased up a bit. Feeling tension leave his shoulders, he unclenched his fists, but the tight jaw remained. The man still did not notice him.

He was followed by a younger version of himself and Rosa-Lee yelped out again. "Manuel, brother!"

"My sister!" He took her away from their father, kissed her soundly on the mouth, and she giggled. When they finally let her go and she stepped back, the two men who caused the dining room to be filled to capacity looked down at her and stopped at her swollen girth.

"Rosie are you in the family way?" Cisco asked, and then he looked up to see Roberto right behind her. His light blue eyes filled with suspicion and surprise.

"Papa, I must introduce you to my husband." She turned around and pulled Roberto closer. Both men's faces turned menacing, especially Manuel's, whose face distorted into an ugly grimace. He stepped in front of her.

"Step aside, sister," he hissed.

"Manuel, you don't understand!"

"What is this pirate doing here?" he demanded.

"He is my husband, Manuel. Papa...?" She turned back to her father with huge eyes, looking for support.

"Manuel, wait, let's hear what is going on." Cisco stopped his son.

"Papa, I love Roberto."

"But child, he kidnapped you."

"Yes, Papa, but he saved my life, mine and Pedro's. Let me explain." Her father looked down at her, his face grim and he touched her shoulder.

"I think we need to go home. Mama is waiting for us. Then you can explain this." He turned his gaze back to Roberto.

"Papa meet Roberto de Ville." She introduced Roberto. Cisco stretched out a paw and Roberto took it, feeling the strength as her father gripped his hand. He almost flinched under the pain but kept his face blank.

"Roberto," Cisco said, "we will talk about this at home."

Roberto nodded. "Yes, Señor." and bowed politely.

†††

The reunion between mother and daughter was heart-warming. Qonchita burst into tears when she saw the state of her daughter. But her face lit as she touched Rosa-Lee's belly with the greatest tenderness and awe. When they introduced her to Roberto, she looked at him, then at her daughter, and saw the love they shared. Without any thought, she pulled him into an embrace and kissed both his cheeks. He could not help but feel elevated by her. He accepted her as a mother into his own life and returned her kindness, much to the dismay of Manuel.

They had a hard time in controlling the young man, who just wanted to floor him at every possible opportunity. Cisco held him in and out of respect for his father, he walked away. He came back later and joined them again.

In the meantime, they read the letter from Pedro, who explained in detail what had happened and the plan they implemented to bring the Falcon down. Slowly Cisco came around, the wary look turning into one of interest.

Deep into the night, five people sat in the study of the Almaida castle as they listened to the unfolding story from Rosa-Lee, who sat next to Roberto, holding his hand.

When they had arrived, he had said he had wanted to explain, but she insisted on doing the talking. Because he knew she knew her family better, he allowed her to proceed.

†††

Pierre and Nora were shown to their suite of rooms and they were already sleeping in the comfortable four-poster bed by the time the others sat down together. Winter was already setting in and they were close to each other in the oversized bed, cuddling. Nora's nausea had finally subsided, and she was feeling like a whole person, to the great joy of her husband. They decided to stay at the Almaida castle until after the birth of their baby before they continued their journey to his house in France.

He had already sent a letter to his mother and sister, informing them of his marriage and the pregnancy and wrote that they would join them before the next winter. He explained that Nora was extremely ill on the voyage and he did not want to cause her or the unborn child any more distress.

†††

When Rosa-Lee finally stopped talking, she smiled up to Roberto, tired but happy, and he smiled, returning his gaze to the Almaida family.

"Señor and Señora, I know we have not met under the best of circumstances, but I really do love your daughter, my Rosa. I have already handed my resignation in, and I plan to become the farmer I always wanted to be. With her at my side, my future is filled with promise." Emotions washed over his face and both the parents could see that this man was genuine in his feelings toward their only daughter.

"I never thought I could have this, a wife and baby to call my own. I vow to look after her and treat her with the utmost love and devotion. She will lead the life she is used to, lacking nothing. My pirate days provided well for me over the years." She squeezed his hand in support. "I love Rosa-Lee. There is no other woman for me." Rosa-Lee wiped away a tear, yawning behind her hand.

"I appreciate your honesty, Roberto." Cisco finally addressed him.

"What you have done for my children put me in your debt and I can see that you really care for Rosa-Lee and love her. I could not have chosen better than you. I understand why you had to come and drag her out of my house like a thief in the night." Roberto flinched under the piercing gaze.

"You are a good man, Señor," Roberto said.

"No, son, just a man who has walked the path and understands much more."

"Thank you, Papa," Rosa-Lee added and yawned again.

"I want to get my wife in bed, if you don't mind."

"Yes, of course, Roberto, she is tired after the long journey. I will have the physician here tomorrow to look at both ladies. In the meantime, son, you are welcome in my family. Cisco raised himself to his full height. His wife followed him. He clasped Roberto's hand in a fatherly gesture.

"Thanks, Señor."

"Papa will be fine, son."

Roberto swallowed at the lump in his throat. *Papa*. When was the last time he had used that word? His eyes misted over, and the man stepped forward and gave him a bear hug.

†††

Later that evening, with the smouldering fire in the hearth creating shadows against the walls and thick curtains, Roberto watched his wife's sleeping form. He brushed away the dark locks covering her beautiful face. The shadows underneath her eyes showed that she had not yet recovered from the journey, but her breathing was slow and at peace. He had one hand on the stretched belly and one hand under her face, the pouty lips warm and inviting. He could not help but smile, tenderly touching the soft skin and tracing every line on the youthful face. A dimpled smile appeared as she cuddled deeper into him.

His Rosa.

All his worries over the last four months were dispelled as utter nonsense. He could only shake his head at his own stupidity. His fretting was in vain and he pulled her closer and closed his eyes. He slept the sleep of a contented man, his world perfect.

Three months later, twins were born to Roberto and Rosa-Lee, a daughter they called Madelyn, after his mother, and a son, Francisco, named after both grandfathers. Roberto was like a proud peacock showing its colourful feathers in a swelled chest. The two children were a true delight to him, and he could not thank her enough for such a joy. He was determined more than ever to be the man his own father had been, with the gracious help of Cisco, who was equally proud of his two grandchildren, spoiling them with gifts.

A month later, Victoria du Val was born, spitting image of her mother, and Pierre was impressed with the beautiful baby who slept soundly in his arms. He wanted to hold her as much as he could because his days with her were almost at an end and he did not want to miss anything right now.

The castle was filled with laughter and baby voices. Both Qonchita and Cisco enjoyed the two couples. The men spoke about their experiences and the women about babies, as well as their up and coming travels to their new homes.

Manuel accepted Roberto reluctantly and, in the end, they departed in good spirits.

Nora and Rosa-Lee became good friends during the voyage and the months at the estate. By the time they departed to their new homes, a journey of just over a week to France, the two women cried. This created a cacophony of distressed cries when the babies joined in, not understanding all the tears. They just knew their mothers were in distress.

The two men had their hands full, calming them all down, and by the time they left, everything was as it should be, in control and at peace. The pirate farmer and his Rosa were content with their new life.

THE END

Thanks for reading my book,
if you enjoyed it, please leave a review at
one or all the links provided.

Many thanks

Author's History

Lynelle Clark is a South African who loves her country, its people, and the rich history.

She has three children, Arline, Odette and Paul, and two grandsons, Nathan and Declan.

She started to write in the beginning of 2010 after she found herself isolated from people and without work.

Her love for reading prompted her to write her own stories, drawing from life's experiences and lessons learned.

She is also presenting Diamant Divas on Elan Global Radio Wednesdays at 10, SA Time. Afrikaans Motivering program vir enkellopende vroue.

Other books from the author

A Pirate's Wife Kindle #Historical #Romance

Amazon: http://amzn.to/1xH8D3M

Smashwords

Bella's Choice

Two roads. One choice.

Anabella Anthony found she was alone in the world at eighteen. Early on, she made a choice; to live an ordinary life away from the lifestyle her parents preferred. However, they had plans for her; they wanted her to become a part of their choices.

All she wanted was a regular household, with normal day to day issues like her peers, parents she could respect, and who above anything else would accept her for the person she is. Torn between dreams that filled her mind with alluring effects and uncomfortable events which tried to sway her, she had to come to a resolution: find peace and stay true to her convictions.

Through it all, she excelled in her sport; a dedicated student who falls in love with a much older man. Will she give in to her body's desires, or will she remain steadfast in her own choices? Can she find the courage to stand amidst the turmoil wanting to drag her down? And most importantly, will she ever forgive those who meant to harm her?

Aldrich Hagin, a lawyer, is ready to settle down. After a tragic loss he experienced right after university he is now, more than ever, ready to move on and start a family. And then he meets a young, energetic, lively woman who turns his life and heart around. Will he be willing to sacrifice his own desires and wait? Can he help her and be the anchor she so desperately need? Confronted with his own decisions, the choice is his as to whether he'll stay or leave. What will he decide?

A love story filled with decisions both have to make; to stand against all odds and remain true to oneself.

Age restriction of 16 is recommended

#Contemporary #Romance #Alternativeliving #Choices

Amazon: http://amzn.to/1H087SK
Smashwords: https://www.smashwords.com/books/view/750384

Blood Mines

Tanya's life was turned upside down when her son, Steve was attacked by renegades and she had to dig deep facing her worst fear to save them both.

It is the year 2048, 30 years after a devastating quake had changed Gauteng's geographic features. The effects of the acid water, that covered most of the area, was visible to everyone but the government. The silent death crawling closer leaving devastation in its path. Nothing is excluded from the terror.

Tanya and Steve's path of survival meet up with the rebels in their search for clean water and she had to face much more than just acid water to stay alive.

A thrilling story of courage and survival.

#Thriller #suspense #futuristic #Environmental #romance #Strongwoman

Group 7 Printers: http://groep7-selfpublish-books.co.za/home/674-blood-mines-lynelle-clark.html
Smashwords: https://www.smashwords.com/books/view/789958
Amazon: https://goo.gl/GgSXGE

To follow:

Goodreads:
http://www.goodreads.com/author/show/6478179.Lynelle_Clark
Amazon:
http://www.amazon.com/gp/profile/AK8O310VW1WEV?e_tf=
1
Twitter: https://twitter.com/LynelleClark1

Blogs:

Inspire to Read: http://lynelleclarkaspiredwriter.blogspot.com/
Vanuit my pen: https://uitmypengse.blogspot.co.za/
Ink in Afrikaans: http://www.ink.org.za/

2 short stories were published in

SA Skrywers Kontreibundel
SA Skrywers Kaleidoskoop
Available at Groep 7 Printers.

Be on the look out for her next book:

Love at War in 2019.

A Military romance / Inspirational story.

www.ingramcontent.com/pod-product-compliance
Lightning Source LLC
Chambersburg PA
CBHW022159170626
46807CB00005B/2269